To Temple Israel
Enjoy reading about
my grandmother's
trip to Texas.
Jan Siegel Hart
2/93

HANNA
THE IMMIGRANT

Hanna and Velvel Astonovitsky, 1906, Russia

HANNA
THE IMMIGRANT

JAN
SIEGEL
HART

EAKIN PRESS ★ Austin, Texas

ISBN 0-89015-805-3

Library of Congress Cataloging-in-Publication Data

Hart, Jan Siegel, 1940–
    Hanna, the immigrant / by Jan Siegel Hart.
        p.   cm.
    Summary: As a Jewish girl growing up in Czarist Russia, Hanna moves
with her family from one village to another and eventually to America.
    ISBN 0-89015-805-3
    [1. Jews — Soviet Union — Fiction. 2. Jews — United States — Fiction.
    3. Emigration and immigration — Fiction.] I. Title.
PZ7.H2567Han   1991
[Fic] — dc20   90-24027
                                                                         CIP
                                                                          AC

To Annie Harelik Novit,
for giving me the love and inspiration
to write her story.

Acknowledgment

Many thanks to Rabbi Kenneth D. Roseman of Temple Shalom in Dallas, Texas, for editing this book.

Contents

Preface

This story began as a family history. My grandmother had such interesting stories to tell that I wanted to share them with others.

Hanna was a ten-year-old Jewish girl in a Russian village at the turn of the century. She began to realize that life was becoming more and more difficult all the time. The czar made many laws which were unfair to the Jews. Jews were only allowed to live in a certain area of Russia called the Pale of Settlement. They were not allowed to own land or practice medicine or law. Only a few could attend universities.

Because of the hard times, many Russian Jews began to leave for a better life in other lands. The port of Galveston, Texas, opened to immigration in 1907. At the age of seventeen, Hanna decided to become a part of the Galveston Movement, and settle in a land where she could start a new life and be free.

1

Hanna Moves Away

Hanna was excited and sad at the same time. She was sad to be leaving her home in the Russian village of Slavan. Behind her were many friends and relatives and cozy, familiar places. Yet Hanna couldn't help being excited too. She wondered what their new home in Parichi would be like, as she bounced along in the horse-drawn wagon.

"Papa, why did we have to move?" Hanna asked. "I liked it in Slavan." She looked at the familiar scenery slipping away.

"Now, Hanna, don't bother Papa with so many questions," Mama said. "You know he had to leave the mill because the czar won't allow Jews to be in control any longer. So Papa can no longer run the mill. And jobs are scarce in Slavan, so we must move on."

Hanna remembered all the times she had walked with her mother and little brothers, Haskell and Morris, to the mill. Many times they had taken Papa's lunch of dark bread, cheese, and a piece of fruit and watched the farmers unload their big wagons overflowing with grain, such as wheat, corn, or rye.

"But I will miss *Bubbye* and *Zayde* and all my friends. Will they come to visit us in Parichi?" Hanna asked sadly.

"I am sure they will, Hanna," Papa answered. "It isn't that far away. And you will make new friends in Parichi. There are many Jews living there. I am sure there must be some Jewish girls who are ten years old." He looked down into Hanna's big blue eyes, which were quickly filling with tears.

"You know Papa has always loved helping you children with your Hebrew lessons. Now Papa's job will be teaching Hebrew to children your age. You will meet many children who will be coming to our house for *cheder*," Mama said.

"Will I be able to take Yiddish and Russian lessons?" Hanna asked, wiping away a tear. She enjoyed learning Yiddish because that was the language all the Jewish people spoke. And, of course, she also needed to know the Russian language. Only boys would be taking Hebrew lessons from Papa. It wasn't considered important for girls to know how to read the prayers in the ancient language of the

Jews. Since there were no free public schools in Russia, Mama and Papa must find new teachers for Hanna. Haskell and Morris would be taught by Papa.

"Hanna, we will make sure you are able to continue your lessons," Papa said. "We have heard there are good teachers in Parichi." Even though there was no money for store-bought toys or clothes for Hanna, there were always rubles for her education.

The wagon had traveled for a long time. Long after it had become dark, Papa gently awakened Hanna. "We are home now. You can finish sleeping tonight in Parichi."

As Hanna rubbed her eyes and stumbled into the tiny house, Mama quickly made sleeping pallets on the floor. As Mama tucked Hanna and her brothers in, she said, "We will say our prayers for the first time in our new home. I pray to God that He grants us health and happiness here."

Then they said their prayers together, first in the ancient language of Hebrew, then in their native tongue: *"Shema Yisroel, Adonoi Eloheinu, Adonoi Echod.* Hear O Israel: The Lord Our God, the Lord is One."

"Good night, my darlings. Sleep well," Mama and Papa said as they kissed each child good night.

As soon as Hanna and her family were settled in their house, Papa began teaching Hebrew. He began with only two students, but, as word spread, parents brought their sons to Papa to learn Hebrew.

3

As soon as Mama had everything unpacked, she began looking for a teacher for Hanna. They had been in Parichi one week when Mama came home with a big smile on her face.

"Hanna, I have found a teacher for you, Mr. Chernov. You may start your lessons next week. And when you get a little older, you may take sewing lessons from his wife. Would you like to do that?"

"Oh yes, Mama. Could I make clothes for myself and for my doll, Ruthe?"

"You certainly may. As soon as you finish your Yiddish and Russian lessons, you may take sewing lessons."

Hanna thought to herself how proud she would be to wear clothes she had sewed by herself. Maybe she would even become good enough to sew for the rest of the family too.

2

The Skaters

Hanna woke to the sound of a baby crying. Three months had passed since the move to Parichi. Now she had a new little brother, David. He was permanently stationed during the day in his crib next to the stove. It was the warmest place in the house, and that is where Mama spent most of her time.

Hanna jumped out of bed and, with fingers flying, dressed quickly. She ran from her cold room to the warmth of the kitchen to help Mama.

"Good morning, Hanna. Could you set the table and pour the milk for yourself and your brothers? I just fed little David, and now I need your help so that I may have our breakfast ready when Papa comes home from *shul*."

There were three synagogues and several churches in Parichi. Even though there were only about 2,000 people living in Parichi, many of them were Jews. Papa, along with the other Jewish men in town, went twice a day to pray at the synagogue. In the early morning hours and again as the sun was setting, he said his prayers of thanks to God.

Just as Hanna finished pouring the milk, Papa came hurrying into the house. "Good morning, Hanna," he said as he tousled her hair and bent down for a kiss. "How is my big girl this morning?"

He walked over to the stove where Mama was dishing out the hot cereal and gave her a kiss. Then he picked David up from his crib and looked at Haskell and Morris. "And how are my boys today?" he asked, tickling David. David gurgled and laughed. Hanna laughed, too, as Haskell and Morris greeted Papa.

"Papa, when I am through with my lessons, may I go watch the ice skaters on the river?" Hanna asked.

"If Mama doesn't need your help this afternoon, then it is all right with me," Papa said as he looked at Mama.

"Hanna, you have been such a good helper all week, you may go watch the skaters today. But you must not go alone. Do you have a friend who can go with you?" Mama asked.

"I will ask Sadie Katzenbaum. She is a girl who is in my class at Mr. Chernov's."

Mama knew that Hanna didn't have many friends in Parichi yet. So she hoped that Sadie could go with Hanna. "If Sadie can't go, then come right home, and we shall find something for you to do."

Mama looked out the window later when it was time for Hanna to come home. It looked very cold. Snow covered everything as far as she could see. But Hanna was nowhere in sight. *She must be with Sadie at the river,* Mama thought.

Even though she wanted Hanna to have some fun, Mama couldn't help worrying about her. Hanna worked very hard helping Mama with the three boys. There was always something to do: cooking, cleaning, clothes to wash. Mama couldn't do it by herself. She wished she could afford to have someone help her, so that Hanna wouldn't have to work so hard. Hanna had always been a good girl, but lately she was becoming very adventurous. She liked to wander around town and explore new places. Mama was afraid she might come to some harm on one of her walks.

While Mama was wondering and worrying about her, Hanna and her friend, Sadie, were running through the woods to get to the beautiful Berezina River. As lovely as it was in the summer, it was even more beautiful in the winter, when it was frozen solid for four months.

As Hanna and Sadie went running through the

snow, they tripped and fell down. Hanna laughed when she looked at Sadie.

"You have snow in your hair, Sadie. You look like an old lady with white hair!" Hanna laughed as she fell back in the snow.

"And you look like a snowman who just got knocked down." Hanna had on so many clothes, she looked very round, like a snowman.

As the girls got up, laughing and brushing off the snow, a big sleigh pulled by two white horses went jingling by. The people in the sleigh waved at them, smiling, and Hanna and Sadie waved back.

They followed the sleigh, skipping through the snow-covered street, to the river. It was beautiful, the sight Hanna had been waiting to see. There were people everywhere. She looked first to the banks of the river, where lumbermen were working, bringing the huge trees they had cut down. Parichi was surrounded by forests, so there were many trees for the lumbermen to cut. In the spring, when the ice melted, three different lumber companies competed for the lumber business on the river. As the river began to flow again, the lumbermen took the logs they had brought to the river, tied them together, and floated them downstream to larger cities, like Bobruysk and Kiev.

Hanna thought about the excitement of seeing the boats come and go on the river as she watched it, now completely frozen. To Hanna, it was a winter wonderland.

"Look, Sadie, everyone in town must be here!"

she said. As they watched the skaters whirl and twirl about on the ice, two ladies skated by, bundled up in coats, hats, gloves, and scarves. Suddenly, they screamed and fell down on the hard, cold ice.

Hanna and Sadie couldn't help themselves. They looked at each other and started to laugh. As they fell back into the snow, tears of laughter were running down their cheeks. This was the most fun of all: watching people who thought they could skate suddenly sit down on the hard ice.

Much later, Hanna realized she was cold and hungry. She and Sadie hurried to their homes for supper. Hanna hoped Mama would not be angry with her for being late.

3

A Sabbath Prayer

As Hanna ran swiftly into the house, slamming the door, Mama turned and said sharply, "I was worried about you. Why were you gone so long?"

"I am sorry I am late, Mama. But we were having such a good time, watching the skaters, I didn't realize how long we were gone." Hanna peeled off her galoshes and hung her coat, gloves, and scarf on a hook by the door to dry.

"Wash up and help set the table. It is almost time for Papa to be home from *shul* and he will want his *Shabbos* meal," Mama said. She looked down at the candlesticks she had polished until they shined brightly. Mama was upset with Hanna for being late. But she was so relieved to have her home safely that she wanted to hug her tightly.

"Yes, Mama," Hanna said as she quickly washed her hands and face and then began to set the table.

Just as Mama was putting the food on the table, Papa came in with a big smile. "Good *Shabbos,* everyone." He took off his coat and hat and made his way around the table, kissing Mama, then Hanna and the boys.

"It is getting dark. Time for Mama to light the *Shabbos* candles," Papa said.

Mama covered her head with a pretty lace kerchief, lit the two candles, and circled her hands around the flames as she said the blessing.

"Blessed are You, O Lord our God, King of the Universe, who has made us holy through Your commandments and commanded us to kindle the Sabbath lights. Amen. Good *Shabbos,* everyone."

"Good *Shabbos,*" they all replied.

After they all gathered around the table, Papa lifted his glass of wine high in the air. "Blessed are You, O Lord our God, King of the Universe, who brings forth fruit of the vine. Amen." Hanna thought to herself that this prayer was a blessing for all the fruits that God gave them. Mama and Papa each took a sip of the wine.

Next Papa uncovered the beautiful braided loaf of *challah* and said, "Blessed are You, O Lord our God, King of the universe, who brings forth bread

12

from the earth. Amen." Again, Hanna thought about this prayer being a blessing for all the food they ate.

Papa cut a piece from the freshly baked *challah* and tore off a piece for himself. Then he passed it to Mama. Each one broke off a piece of the still-warm bread, then passed it around until baby David got the last tiny piece. He promptly stuck it in his mouth and sucked on it until it got soft enough to swallow.

Now Mama filled the plates with meat and potatoes and cabbage which had been cooked together and smelled wonderful. A piece of *challah* was added to each plate. Hanna was so hungry! She received her plate and quickly began eating. She made her fork fly from her plate to her mouth until her plate was clean.

This was, indeed, a special meal. Hanna's family, along with their Jewish neighbors, could not afford to buy meat very often. During the week, Mama cooked delicious meals of soup, bread, potatoes, and cabbage. Always on the Sabbath they celebrated with meat, special foods, and their best tablecloth.

As they ate their Sabbath meal, each one told something that had happened to them that day. Papa got a new student, bringing his total up to twelve. Mama finished embroidering the new *challah* cover. She also told them the news from Slavan which she received in a letter from *Bubbye* and *Zayde*.

Both Hanna's parents, Baila and Max, were

from families named Gorelik. They were not related, even though there were many Goreliks in town. Many Jews took the names of the towns from which they came. The story told was that when the town was burned during a pogrom, all the government papers were burned too. After that, the town was known as Gorelik, which means burned down.

Haskell and Morris made a new friend who liked to play their special game of chase. Hanna told about the hundreds of skaters on the river, especially the ones who fell down. Mama and Papa looked at each other and tried not to laugh as Hanna described their neighbor, Mrs. Dubrovnik. How red her face got when she joined the many who struggled to get up after falling on the hard ice!

Hanna always got a warm feeling as they sat and ate and talked while the Sabbath candles burned down and gave their final sputter before going out. Hanna thought, *Maybe Parichi won't be so bad after all.*

4

The Lights of Chanukah

The next week, Hanna began celebrating the eight days of *Chanukah*. Mama always invited all their relatives for the first night and prepared a special meal. It was a festive, joyful holiday. Hanna looked forward to seeing her grandparents and aunts, uncles and cousins. She helped Mama pluck the goose because she loved *gribenehs*. Mama removed the fat from the goose, melted it down slowly over the fire, then added chopped onions and cooked them until they were brown. Hanna licked her lips while it cooked.

As the goose was cooking, Hanna helped Mama grate all the potatoes for the *latkes*. She chopped onions, added them along with eggs to the potatoes, and dropped spoonfuls of the mixture into the hot grease. It spattered and sizzled while it cooked. Hanna felt very proud to be cooking alongside Mama. She was getting hungry, smelling all the delicious foods.

Before she knew it, Papa was home, and their little house had filled with relatives.

"It is time to light the first candle of *Chanukah*," Papa said. Everyone gathered around the *menorah* and recited the blessings of *Chanukah*.

"Blessed are You, O Lord our God, King of the universe, who has sanctified us by Your commandments and commanded us to kindle the lights of *Chanukah*. Amen."

"Blessed are You, O Lord our God, King of the universe, who made miracles for our fathers in days of old at this time of year. Amen."

There was a third prayer, a special one for the first night of *Chanukah*. "Blessed are You, O Lord our God, King of the universe, who kept us alive and sustained us and brought us to this joyful season. Amen."

Papa lit the small candle in the top of the *menorah*. Then, he used it to light the first candle for the first night of *Chanukah*. Everyone said, "Happy *Chanukah*."

"And now we eat," Papa said after he recited the blessing for the food.

Everyone was talking and laughing and filling their plates at the same time. Mama had made applesauce from the apples that had grown on the trees

16

in their yard. It was the perfect topping for the potato *latkes*. After dinner, everyone had hot tea from
the samovar, sweetened with homemade jelly from
the fruit Hanna and her brothers had picked from
their cherry trees.

"It is delicious, Mama," Hanna exclaimed.

On the first night, Papa always told the story of
Chanukah. Hanna never tired of hearing how the
tiny band of soldiers won their battle against the
Syrians many years ago. When the eternal light was
lit during the rededication of the Temple, the tiny
bottle of oil was only enough for one day. But it
burned miraculously for eight days. That is why
Chanukah is celebrated for eight days, and that is
why Hanna and her family, like other Jews, lit another candle every evening until eight burned
brightly.

Hanna and her brothers and cousins were given
gifts of *Chanukah gelt* and hand-carved *dreidels*.
The children sang and spun their *dreidels,* playing
the lively game until it was very late. Hanna was
having an especially good time because she was win-
ning the game. But it was time for bed, and everyone
kissed and hugged and said their goodbyes.

After everyone had left, Mama and Papa
brought out a special gift wrapped in tissue paper
and handed it to Hanna. "Happy *Chanukah*,
Hanna," they said.

"Thank you," Hanna said as she tore off the

paper. Inside was a brightly colored, hand-knitted scarf and matching gloves.

"Your old ones were getting very shabby. Take good care of these and don't lose them," Mama said.

"Yes, Mama. I love *Chanukah* time," Hanna said sleepily as Papa tucked her into bed.

5

Something Unexpected

Hanna awoke to the lovely fragrance of cherry blossoms. Spring had arrived, and she looked out her window to see the cherry trees filled with blossoms. The cherry and apple trees were in abundance in their back yard. Hanna didn't know which she liked best: the blossoms, eating the fruit right off the tree, or eating the applesauce, jams, and pies Mama made from the fresh fruit.

As Hanna came into the kitchen, Mama was feeding the boys. "Hanna, please help get breakfast ready for Papa. I need your help more than ever, now that we have little David." Since Hanna was the oldest child, and a girl besides, she was expected to help with the younger children. Most of the time she didn't mind. But sometimes she just wanted to play all day and forget that she had little brothers.

"*Bubbye* is coming today to help us get ready for *Pesach*. With little David to take care of, I don't have time to clean and do all the special cooking," Mama said.

"I will help you and *Bubbye*," Hanna said. "I can help *Bubbye* make pies." When *Bubbye* came to visit, she always made some of her special apricot pies. Hanna enjoyed helping pinch the dough together so that the juicy filling didn't come sizzling out while it cooked.

"*Bubbye* won't be making pies this time," Mama said. Hanna had forgotten that Jews don't eat leavened products on *Pesach,* including crusts.

"There are other holiday foods to be prepared. So don't dawdle on the way home from your lessons," Mama said.

Hanna knew that Mama didn't mean to be abrupt with her. Mama had a lot to do and was very tired. Not only did she have the usual duties of a wife and mother, of keeping her family clothed and fed, but Mama was very religious. She kept a *kosher* kitchen, which involved separate dishes for meat and milk products. She believed the strict observance of dietary rules made her family stronger in their Jewish beliefs.

During *Pesach,* or Passover, there was much work to be done. Mama wanted to clean the house from top to bottom to prepare for the special holiday. There were separate dishes used only for *Pesach.*

Special foods were prepared for the *Seder,* the combination meal and religious service.

Hanna set the table for breakfast. When Papa came in, she dished out his hot cereal. After breakfast, she hurried to her lessons with thoughts of *Bubbye* and *Zayde* and all the wonderful foods that would soon be prepared.

After school, Hanna walked home with Sadie to see what preparations were taking place there. Sadie's *Bubbye* was also visiting. As soon as they walked in the kitchen door, Mrs. Katzenbaum shooed them out. It looked like a storm had hit. All the dishes, pots and pans, and utensils were being washed and dried. All traces of bread were being cleaned away to prepare for the eight days of eating *matzo* instead of bread. Sadie and Hanna giggled and ran to Sadie's room.

"I am glad *Bubbye* is here to help Mama," Sadie said. "If not, I would have to help clean the kitchen."

"Me too," agreed Hanna. "My *Bubbye* is coming to help my Mama today. When I grow up, I am not going to go to all that trouble for holidays. Mama is tired all the time and never has time to play with me anymore. She used to make pretty clothes for me, but since David came, she has no time for me at all."

"When I grow up I am going to get married, but I shall never have babies. They are too messy!" Sadie exclaimed. "When I grow up I am going to marry a tall, handsome man who has lots of money. He will buy me a piano and after I learn to play, I shall give piano lessons to all the little girls in town.

The boys are busy with their Hebrew lessons, so the girls will have time to learn to play the piano." She folded her arms, pleased with herself.

Hanna clapped her hands. "Oh, that is a wonderful idea. I wish I had a piano. If I could play the piano, I would play for Mama and Papa every evening."

"Sadie, come to the kitchen and help us put things away," Mrs. Katzenbaum called.

"Well, it looks like it is time for me to go home," Hanna said. "I shall see you tomorrow."

"Goodbye," called Sadie as Hanna ran to get her coat and books. "See you tomorrow."

The sun shone down on Hanna, and she smiled. It was a crisp, clear day with just a hint of spring in the air. As she skipped down the dirt street, she thought to herself: *I am going to take a different way home today. There will be plenty for me to do when I get home. I might as well enjoy this pretty day while I can.*

Turning down a strange street, she saw a group of older boys coming toward her. There were no Jews living on this street. But Hanna was not concerned. There were many Russian families who lived near her, and they got along fine.

As they got closer, the boys stared at her. They said something to each other. Then they started to smile. One boy whistled a Russian tune. Just as they were about to pass, two of the boys stepped in front of her.

"Where are you going, little girl?" the tall, thin boy asked.

"Home," said Hanna, and she started to step around them.

"The little Jew girl is going home," taunted the red-haired boy.

"You don't want to go home just yet," said the pudgy boy with a scowl.

"Yes, I do," said Hanna. Her heart was thumping loudly, and she was trying to keep from crying. She started again to pass around the boys, but they quickly stepped in front of her, knocking her down. As she got up, she began to cry. She couldn't hold back the tears any longer. "Please let me go," she pleaded.

"Well, we wouldn't want to keep the little Jew girl from going to her dirty little Jew home, would we, fellows?" sneered the red-headed boy.

The tall boy stared down at her. "Go ahead. Get out of here. And stay in your own neighborhood. We don't want ours dirtied up with Jews."

Hanna started to run. She could hear the laughter of the boys growing fainter and fainter. She didn't even notice when she dropped her scarf and gloves that Mama had knitted for her. She didn't stop running until she reached home.

6

A Passover Seder

As Hanna lay in bed that night, she listened to the conversation going on in the next room.

"I can't believe that it happened in our own town!" cried Mama. "When she came in with her clothes all dirty, I knew something was wrong — even before I saw her face all stained with tears. How could they have been so cruel?" Mama choked back her tears of fury and frustration.

"I have heard of worse things happening in the cities of Minsk and Bobruysk," Papa said. "People have had rocks thrown through their windows. Their businesses have been burned. If they try to stop it, they are beaten. Worst of all, after "JEW" is written on their stores, people are afraid to shop there, and they are forced out of business. I am afraid this evil is spreading throughout our country, perhaps throughout Europe. I don't know what we can do to stop it."

"Maybe if we ignore it, it will go away," replied Mama. "We get along fine with our Russian neighbors. We respect their way of life, and they respect ours. Why, we have even hired some of them to work for us, chopping wood and tilling the garden. They were glad to do it for us, and we were glad to pay them for it."

"That is right, Mama, but there is something in the air that I fear will not go away. We shall just have to be prepared for more of this treatment and do the best we can to get along," said Papa sadly.

"Tomorrow night is the Passover *Seder*. We must pray to God to help us find joy and hope to celebrate this year."

After that, all was quiet in the house as Mama and Papa thought their own private thoughts.

The next morning, nothing more was said of the incident. There were no lessons this day so that everyone could prepare for *Pesach*. Hanna was quiet, not her usual bubbly self, but she helped, as always, with breakfast. After breakfast, Papa went to the bakery to pick up the *matzo* for *Pesach*. Mama and *Bubbye* began to cook for the *Seder*. While Mama grated the horseradish root, she kept wiping her eyes because it smelled very strong. Every once in a while, she ran to the window and opened it for a breath of fresh air. *Bubbye,* meanwhile, was busy peeling and chopping apples and nuts for the *charoses*. The chicken soup had been made the day before, along with the *matzo* balls, which would bob and float in the soup. Today, a goose would be roasted to a golden brown and vegetables would complete the meal. This was the biggest and fanciest meal of the whole year. Everyone looked forward to being together for this special festival meal.

It was Hanna's job to set the festival table and fill the *Seder* plate with foods which represented things in the story of *Pesach*. As she did this, she tried to remember from last year what each food meant. Finally, she asked *Bubbye* to help her, even though she knew it would all be explained at the service that night.

"*Bubbye,* tell me what all the foods mean. I remember that the *moror,* or horseradish, represents the bitter life of slavery in Egypt. But I don't remember all the rest. Will you tell me?" Hanna asked imploringly of *Bubbye*.

"Hanna, you are just full of questions today, aren't you? Since I have always told you that the best way to learn is to ask questions, I guess I had better provide some answers." *Bubbye* chuckled to herself and shook her head. "Now, let me see if I can explain them. The bone of roast lamb is a reminder of the offering that was brought to the holy Temple in Jerusalem a long time ago."

Bubbye then pointed to the egg and said, "The roasted hard-boiled egg is a symbol of life."

Picking up a sprig of parsley, *Bubbye* said, "The

sprig of parsley is a reminder that this is a spring festival. The salt water in which we dip the parsley recalls the salty tears the Israelites shed when they were slaves. The *charoses* that I am making represents the bricks and mortar with which Jewish slaves built the palaces and monuments of the Egyptian kings. Now, are there any more questions?"

"Yes, *Bubbye,* one more. Papa is bringing *matzo* home today. Why do we eat it instead of bread?" Hanna asked.

"When the enslaved Jews were finally allowed to leave Egypt, they were in such a hurry, they didn't have time to let their dough rise. So when they baked the loaves of unleavened bread, they came out flat. We eat *matzo* to remind us of those times," *Bubbye* said as she gave Hanna a hug. "Now, if there are no more questions, you need to finish setting the table, while I finish making the *charoses.*"

"Thank you, *Bubbye.*" Hanna had more questions, but she didn't feel like asking them. She wanted to know why those boys were so mean to her. Why did they call her names, when they didn't even know her? Why should they hate her just because they were of different religions? Hanna had many questions that Mama and Papa had not been able to answer the night before. She shook her head as if to clear it. She didn't want to think of such things today.

The sun was starting to go down. Hanna and her brothers were through with their chores and were eating a snack in the kitchen. The door opened, and a cold gust of air blew in, followed by Papa and *Zayde*.

"What is this? Have the children started the *Seder* without us?" Papa asked with a twinkle in his eye.

"No, Papa," Hanna said, as she and her brothers swarmed around him and *Zayde* for their hugs and kisses.

"The service is so long that it is hard for the little ones to wait for the meal. This should tide them over so they won't get fidgety during the service," Mama said. "By the time you wash up, we shall be ready."

As everyone washed their hands, Mama and *Bubbye* put the food on the table. Then they took off their aprons.

"Come everyone. Sit down. Let's get started," *Bubbye* called.

All the family were dressed in their best clothes. Hanna had on a pretty dress Mama had made for her last year. It had pink and red flowers and a big white collar. She still loved it, even though it was getting tight.

After everyone was assembled around the table, Mama lit the candles and said a prayer. Then Papa said the prayers over all the holiday foods. The youngest child was supposed to ask the four questions about the holiday. Since David was too little, the next youngest, Morris, was asked to participate in the service. With some help from *Zayde,* he asked questions relating to *Pesach*. Papa answered the questions and explained the story of the exodus of the Jews from Egypt. At the appointed time in the service, everyone sipped the homemade *Pesach* wine. This year Hanna got to drink wine for the first time, while the boys still had grape juice in their glasses.

Hanna was getting very tired. Her chair seemed to be getting harder and harder. But, finally, the prayers were finished, and the food was served. This was Hanna's favorite part of the evening. She waited all year for Mama's *matzo* ball soup. It was as good as she remembered.

"Mama, you have outdone yourself again this year. Everything was delicious." Papa wiped his mouth, then patted his stomach to show how full he was. "But it looks like the *Seder* was too long for the little ones."

Haskell and Morris had laid their heads down and gone to sleep at the table. Hanna's eyelids were getting very heavy. The baby had slept through the whole evening.

Mama and Papa got up, Papa picking up Haskell and Mama picking up Morris. "Come along, Hanna. Say good night. It is time for bed," Mama said as she looked back over her shoulder.

"Good night, *Bubbye*. Good night, *Zayde*," Hanna said, as she kissed them both.

"Good night and a good *Pesach* to you," they both said, giving her hugs and kisses.

Hanna put on her gown. She fell into bed and was soon fast asleep.

7

The Sewing Lessons

Two years had gone by. Hanna had just celebrated her twelfth birthday. Mama gave a big party
for her friends. *Bubbye* and *Zayde* came too. It was a
special time, and Hanna's family realized she was
growing up.

Hanna sat on her bed with Sadie, looking at her
birthday gifts. Her friends had given her books and
many colored ribbons for her hair. She was letting
her long brown hair hang freely now that she was
getting older. She was tiring of paper dolls and braided hair.

"Look at these ribbons, Sadie. They are in every
color. Aren't they pretty?" Hanna held up the ribbons, making them dance in the air.

·They will look so pretty in your hair," said Sadie. "The blue one matches your dress. Now, that is perfect," she said as she tied Hanna's thick hair up with the ribbon.

"And the yellow one matches your dress," Hanna said, tying Sadie's red curls up with the ribbon. "Now we are ready for another party," she laughed.

Sadie picked up a book and flipped the pages. "May I read this when you are through with it?" she asked.

"Of course, Sadie. You may read any of my new books. You have read all my other books. It is a good thing I got some new ones!" Hanna and Sadie laughed together.

Hanna enjoyed reading occasionally, but Sadie devoured every book she could get her hands on. The subject didn't really matter. She seemed to lose herself in whatever she was reading. She enjoyed living through the stories. They took her away from her everyday life in Parichi to new and exciting places. Sometimes Hanna had trouble getting her to do anything else but read.

Hanna stroked some brightly colored material. Along with the material, Mama and Papa had given Hanna her own needles, thread, scissors, and pin cushion filled with pins. Best of all, she would start taking sewing lessons from Mrs. Chernov.

"Look at the pretty sewing basket, Sadie. I can't wait to start sewing. Soon I shall have new clothes I have sewed myself," Hanna said as she put all her sewing supplies lovingly into the basket decorated with lace and ribbons. "How did *Bubbye* and *Zayde* know just what I would need?"

"Your parents told them, you silly goose," laughed Sadie.

Hanna was very excited to be starting her sewing lessons at last. Mama had taught her how to do handwork, to crochet and to do simple things like sew on buttons and hem dresses. But Hanna had never sewed anything completely by herself. It was very exciting to learn to operate a sewing machine.

"I am glad to be finished with Yiddish and Russian lessons. Now I can start learning to do something I can use to make a living. When I am good enough, I want to sew for my family and friends. When people see how good I sew, they will bring their business to me," Hanna said, gazing dreamily out the window.

"I admire you, Hanna, for having plans for your future and doing something to make your dreams come true. I guess I am lazy. I would just like to read all day. Someday, when my handsome prince comes, he will take me away from Parichi to his castle and give me everything I always wanted."

"Oh, Sadie, you are a dreamer. You are not lazy. So what if you don't like to cook and do things around the house? You have read more books than anyone I know. I admire you for that," said Hanna.

"I guess that is why we stay good friends. We bring out the best in each other," Sadie said as she hugged Hanna. "Now I have to go home. It was a lovely party. Many more happy birthdays!"

"Goodbye, Sadie. Thank you for the book." Hanna waved as Sadie went flying out the door.

The next day Hanna woke and hurried to dress. This was the day of her first sewing lesson. She checked her sewing basket for the tenth time, and, sure enough, everything was still there, neatly in place.

After breakfast, she kissed Mama goodbye, picked up her sewing basket, and headed to the Chernovs' house.

When she arrived, Mrs. Chernov greeted Hanna at the door with a smile. "Hello, Mrs. Chernov," Hanna said.

"Good morning, Hanna. Did you have a happy birthday?" Mrs. Chernov helped her with her coat and then motioned her to take a seat.

"Yes, I did. I got all these gifts to prepare me for sewing lessons." Hanna showed Mrs. Chernov her basket filled with sewing supplies and material.

"That is wonderful, Hanna. Your Mama tells me that you have learned to do some handwork, and now you want to learn to make your own clothes on a sewing machine."

"That is right. Can I start sewing on my dress today?" asked Hanna.

"Let's not be in too big a hurry. You need to learn some basic rules before you begin a large project like that. I shall show you how to measure and make a pattern, how to cut the material, and how to use the sewing machine, all in good time," Mrs. Chernov explained.

Hanna looked down at the floor, her face filled with disappointment. She had hoped to start sewing a dress today.

"You may watch me while I finish sewing this shirt for my neighbor, Mrs. Dubrovnik." As Mrs. Chernov pedaled, the machine made the final stitches in the shirt.

Hanna sat, looking in wonder at the machine. She had never seen a sewing machine before. All her clothes had been stitched by hand by Mama or *Bubbye*.

"How fast you sew, Mrs. Chernov. It would take Mama much longer to do what you just did so quickly. Will I be able to do that too?" asked Hanna.

"All in good time, Hanna. Sewing is an art. It requires patience and concentration. Take as much care with your work as if it were a piece of art. If you make a mistake, rip it out!" said Mrs. Chernov with a flip of her hand.

"Mrs. Chernov, when shall I get to use the sewing machine?" Hanna asked.

"I can see that you are anxious to learn," chuckled Mrs. Chernov. "Go to my piecebag and find something to practice on."

Hanna ran to the piecebag and found a small piece of blue and white calico that she recognized from Mrs. Chernov's dress. "May I use this?" Hanna asked.

"Yes, bring it here, Hanna. I shall show you how

to sew on the material while you pedal the machine." Mrs. Chernov moved over to make room for Hanna's chair. Together, they sewed Hanna's first stitches on the sewing machine.

At supper that night, Hanna had so much to tell and was so excited, she could hardly stop to catch her breath.

"It sounds like you had an interesting day," said Papa. "When may we expect to see you wearing a new dress?" he asked as he winked at Mama.

"Not for a long time. Mrs. Chernov says I have many things to learn before I am ready for a big project like that. I shall start by making pillowcases. After I sew them, I shall learn to do a flower design with embroidery."

Even though Hanna was excited, Mama could tell Hanna was also disappointed that it would take so long before she could make a dress. Hanna had found that there was a lot more to sewing than she realized. But Mama also knew that Hanna was determined to learn and would find the patience to become a good seamstress.

8

Mama's and Papa's Surprise

Three years had passed, and Hanna was fifteen years old. She was returning home from delivering a dress she had made for a neighbor. The two years she had spent sewing with Mrs. Chernov had been rewarding. This year, Hanna had been sewing by herself. She had saved her money and bought Mrs. Chernov's old sewing machine. Mrs. Chernov had earned enough money to buy a new one. Hanna couldn't have been happier if it had been brand new. It still sewed as smoothly as a skater gliding across the ice. Since it was the machine Hanna had learned to sew on, it was like an old friend.

As Hanna came into the yard, her brothers called out, "Hanna, come play hopscotch with us."

"I can't right now, maybe later," she said, opening the door. She smiled to herself. She had taught her brothers to play hopscotch one day when she and Sadie were playing. Her brothers had pestered her for a long time before she finally allowed them to play. Now they enjoyed playing hopscotch as much as stick ball.

Mama and Papa were studying some papers at the kitchen table. "Tell us what you think, Hanna," said Papa.

"What is this?" asked Hanna as she sat down in a chair and peered at the drawings.

"These are drawings of our new house. This is the kitchen. There will be plenty of cabinets for all my dishes. Here is the parlor where we shall entertain our guests. And here is Papa's library. There will be shelves for all his books along this wall, and there is plenty of room for a table and chairs for his students."

"Oh, Mama. How wonderful! I didn't know you were planning a new house. Where is my room?" Hanna asked, her eyes scanning the drawings.

"This is something Papa and I have wanted for a long time. I can hardly believe it is really going to happen. We shall finally have enough room!" Mama said.

"So, you want to know where your room is," said Papa. "Well, now, here is our room and here is the boys' room. So this room must be yours." Papa smiled and pointed to a corner square on the paper.

"Oh, it looks big. I shall have plenty of room for my sewing machine and supplies. Now my customers will be able to come for a fitting, and there will be room for them to change." Tears of happiness were starting to form in Hanna's eyes. "Thank you, Mama," she said with a kiss and a hug. "Thank you, Papa," she repeated, throwing her arms around Papa. "It is wonderful, just wonderful! Where is it to be built? May I tell Sadie?"

"So many questions!" laughed Mama. "Yes, you may tell. It will be no secret when the carpenters start work on it next week. It will be in the next block on the vacant lot next to the Abramowitz house."

"Goodbye. I will be home in time for supper." In a flash Hanna was out the door, almost knocking down her brothers in her haste.

When Hanna arrived at the Katzenbaums' house, Sadie was reading. Sadie had to get Hanna to calm down and repeat everything again before she was able to understand about the new house plans.

"That is lovely, Hanna. I am very happy for you and your family." Sadie hugged Hanna.

"Let's go look at the lot where the house will be built," said Hanna.

The girls ran to the kitchen to find Sadie's mother. Hanna told Mrs. Katzenbaum the good news about the new house. "I am very happy for your family, Hanna. But Sadie can't go with you now. She promised to help me with the baking. Maybe tomorrow she can go with you. I know she would much rather be anywhere else but in this kitchen." Sadie looked embarrassed as her mother hugged her.

Hanna knew this was true. Hanna complained about helping her mother too, but she truly loved to cook. She was almost as good a cook as her mother. She felt a sense of pride when the family complimented her cooking. Over the years, Hanna had watched Mama carefully and learned how to cook, as well as how to keep the house shining clean. Mama really depended on her help and didn't need to tell her how to do things anymore.

On the way to the vacant lot, Hanna stopped and sat under a tree to think. The hill looked down on the town of Parichi. She watched the girls from the Russian Orthodox Church school. They were her age and younger, all dressed alike in drab brown dresses. They lived in dormitories. Some of the girls came from far away for their education at the boarding school. As Hanna watched them march from one building to another, she thought how different their lives were, even though they lived so close to one another.

Hanna often came to this spot to think when the noise of her brothers became too much for her. She had discovered this spot shortly after the move to Parichi. Today, she thought back over the three years she had spent learning her craft of sewing. She thought of the many long hours spent bending over the machine by the light of the kerosene lamp. She thought of the many pricked fingers and of the times

she had to rip out her work and how frustrating it had been. But she was proud of her work now.

So many women were bringing their sewing to her, she couldn't do it all. News traveled fast in their little town. Women were happy to pay her a reasonable price for clothing which was well-fitted and well-sewn. Maybe Hanna could get some girls to help her. She decided to talk to Mrs. Chernov about it. Maybe she would know of someone who would like to earn a little money by sewing.

By the time Hanna got home, Mama was getting upset and worried about her. Ever since the incident with the Russian boys so many years before, Mama became concerned when Hanna was gone very long.

The talk at supper that night was all about the house. Haskell, Morris, and David were just as excited as Hanna.

"We found a contractor to build it at a reasonable price," explained Papa. "It should be finished in two months. The first thing we will do is plant a tree, an apple tree."

"And we will watch it grow just as we have watched our children grow," said Mama.

The next week, the house was started. Every day the Goreliks would walk the block to the new house and watch it take shape and grow. Sometimes they would take water to the men working on the house. Hanna had met all the workers. One was a young man of seventeen, the son of the contractor,

Haskell Astonovitsky. His name was Velvel. He had just finished his studies at a *yeshiva* and was now working his first full-time job as a carpenter for his father. Hanna never said much to the workers, but she always let them know when she brought water for them, and they thanked her.

Like the house, Hanna's business was growing too. Mrs. Chernov gave Hanna the names of some of her best pupils. Hanna talked to a girl named Rebecca about working for her. Rebecca came to the Goreliks' house one day with a blouse she had completed.

"You do very nice work, Rebecca," said Hanna. "If you would like to continue sewing for me, I would be happy to pay you."

Rebecca was just a little younger than Hanna. She was delighted to be able to earn some money of her own. She told Hanna she was saving her money.

"What are you going to do with your money?" asked Hanna.

"I am saving it to go to America," said Rebecca. "My aunt and uncle have been there for a year. They write letters telling us that we should join them."

"What is it like in America?" asked Hanna.

"My aunt and uncle work very hard sewing night and day," said Rebecca. "But they have freedom there. There are free schools for their children. There is no czar to tell them how to live or where to live. My cousins are studying during the day in school and sewing at night to earn money. At least there are possibilities for a better life there."

That night Hanna told her parents about the conversation with Rebecca. Mama and Papa knew some people who had gone to America. They told Hanna and the boys stories they had heard about some of the people who had immigrated to New York City.

"I am not interested in moving to a country where I don't know the language. How would we get along?" wondered Papa. "Things could go wrong there too. How do we know these people who immigrated aren't just telling us these stories because they are embarrassed to admit they made a mistake?"

As Hanna lay in bed that night, she had a lot to think about. Even though her sewing business was doing well, how successful could she expect to be in Parichi? How could she get that nice young man to talk to her? If he was as shy around girls as she was around boys, they might never get to know each other!

9

A New Friend

"Hanna, Mrs. Erenburg is here for a fitting."
Mama welcomed the short, gray-haired woman into
the parlor as she called to Hanna.

Hanna got up from her sewing machine and
greeted Mrs. Erenburg as she walked into the parlor. This was the third time Mrs. Erenburg had come
to Hanna to have a garment made.

"Mrs. Erenburg, I was just finishing the pattern
for your new dress. You can choose from three styles
I have designed for you. One has a small collar like
the last dress I made for you." Hanna took Mrs. Erenburg by the hand and led her back to her room.

"Hanna, you did such a beautiful job of sewing
that dress, I would like this one to be just like it, but

of a different material. My sister sent this material from Kiev. Isn't it lovely?"

Mrs. Erenburg opened the package and took out some pale yellow fabric. "Do you have thread to match it?" she asked.

"I am sure I can find some to match. This is good material . . . it should look very nice on you," Hanna said as she felt the material.

As Hanna's business grew, she learned to design patterns for her customers. She had been bored sewing the same styles over and over again and she enjoyed being creative in her dress designs. Her customers appreciated this and rewarded her by returning again and again and by sending their friends to her as well.

"Hanna, you must be pleased to be in this new house. It is much larger than the old house," Mrs. Erenburg said as she looked around Hanna's room for the first time.

"Oh, I am so happy to have my sewing corner in my own room now. I can sew until late at night and not disturb the rest of the family." Hanna began to pin the pattern on Mrs. Erenburg. "This will give you an idea of what this larger sleeve will look like."

"My dear, you had better measure me again. I may be larger than the last time I was here." Mrs. Erenburg looked into the mirror.

"Now, Mrs. Erenburg, you don't look any larger. But I will take your measurements again to be sure." Hanna took her tape measure from around her neck, where it rested most of the day.

After Mrs. Erenburg had gone, Mama stopped at the door of Hanna's room. "Another satisfied customer, Hanna?"

"Yes, Mama. And it was a good thing I measured her again. If she gains any more weight, I will have to let out all her clothes." Hanna laughed. "I didn't tell her that her measurements were larger this time. She would have been very unhappy."

"You certainly don't have to worry about growing out of your clothes. You don't eat enough to keep a bird alive," said Mama.

"Mama, you always want me to eat. I eat enough," Hanna said.

"But that is my job. You know that." Mama and Hanna laughed.

"Mama, I made you a new scarf to match the new blouse you are wearing." Hanna held out the scarf as Mama took off the old one.

"You are spoiling me, my dearest daughter," Mama said, tying the new scarf around her head.

"You are only saying that because I am your only daughter," laughed Hanna.

As Hanna looked at her mother, she thought, *How beautiful she is. It is a shame she has to wear a* sheitel. *It is made of her own hair, long, shiny and brown, the same color as mine.*

"When I get married, will I have to shave my head and wear a *sheitel* if I don't want to?" Hanna asked.

"It is the tradition, Hanna. I expect you to follow the traditions of our people," Mama replied.

47

"We have many traditions which are beautiful. I especially enjoy the holiday traditions. But what is the reason all married Jewish women must cut their hair and wear a *sheitel*?" asked Hanna.

"The rabbis tell us that once a woman is married, her hair, her crowning beauty, must not be visible so it does not distract men from their prayers," Mama explained.

"I have heard that in America married women don't cover their hair, except with a shawl," Hanna said.

"Well, that is America and this is Russia." Mama turned and went back to her work in the kitchen. Hanna knew Mama was not happy that she had questioned a Jewish tradition. She was expected to accept all traditions without question.

That evening, as Mama and Hanna were cleaning up after supper, Papa mentioned that he would have a visitor later. A young man wanted to borrow one of his books. This was not unusual. Papa often had people stop by to borrow books. Lately, more people than ever came to the house, many of them just to see his new library. The Goreliks' house was not larger than their neighbors' houses, but it did have the largest library. Papa loved to argue topics of religion. He would pull a book from the shelf and open it to a well-read page. He usually was able to prove his point by referring to one of his books.

Later, as the family sat in the parlor, there was a knock at the door. Papa opened it and greeted his guest. Hanna saw that it was Velvel Astonovitsky.

Everyone said hello, then Papa and Velvel went into the library. After a while, they returned to the parlor with several books. Hanna and Mama were working on their embroidery. The boys had gone to their room.

As Velvel read, occasionally the book slipped down, and he was able to study Hanna. As Hanna worked, she would sometimes lift her eyes. There he would be, looking at her! Hanna felt her face get red. She knew she was blushing, but she couldn't do anything about it.

After that night, Velvel came often to the Goreliks' house to borrow books. Hanna never said more than hello and goodbye. Velvel would sit in the parlor reading a book, but very often as Hanna watched him, the book would slip down, and their eyes would meet. Hanna would blush.

One evening, after several months of these visits, Papa and Velvel got into a heated discussion about working people. Since there was no limit on the amount of hours people worked, they often worked until 11:00 or 12:00 at night. The workers had recently organized and begun to put pressure on their employers and the government for better working conditions. Many of the workers were children. Some of them ruined their health or even died in accidents because they were tired or the work was dangerous. Velvel was a young man who got involved in causes in which he believed. Papa argued that he shouldn't call attention to himself. If the czar got angry with these young people, there could be more burnings and beatings.

Hanna listened with great interest to the conversation. She had heard of these organizations. She too believed that by organizing, people could bring about better working conditions for themselves.

The next day Hanna told Sadie about the conversation between Papa and Velvel.

Sadie said, "There is a meeting tonight at the Bernsteins'. Why don't we go?"

"I don't know if Mama and Papa will allow me to go," said Hanna.

"If you tell them we are going together, they might. Don't you think it would be interesting? Maybe Velvel will be there." Sadie raised her eyebrows in a questioning look.

"It is worth a try. What time is the meeting?" asked Hanna.

"It is at seven o'clock. If you can go, be here fifteen minutes before and we will walk together. I hope you can go. I think my parents will let me attend. They have been talking about these meetings. They are proud of the young people who are taking a stand for their rights," Sadie said.

At exactly 6:45, Hanna knocked at the Katzenbaums' door. Sadie was waiting for her. The Bernsteins lived only a few blocks away. When they arrived, the front room was filled with people. Most of them Hanna had seen before, but she didn't really know them. Hanna and Sadie took a seat on the floor. A young man named Sol led the meeting. He explained the immediate goal of the workers' organization was to shorten the workday in the factories. "If more people were involved, we would have a better chance of reaching our goals," he said.

As Hanna and Sadie were getting ready to leave, someone called to Hanna. She turned around, and there stood Velvel.

"Good evening, Hanna," he said. "I didn't know you were interested in the cause of the workers."

"Hello, Velvel. I didn't see you when I came in. There were so many people!"

"I was standing just outside the door, so that I could hear what was going on," he said.

"I am very interested in the cause of the workers. After all, soon my brothers may be working in factories. I want all of them to have a better life," Hanna explained.

"I am glad to hear that," said Velvel. "Maybe I will see you at another meeting."

Hanna's heart was pounding so loudly, she just knew that Velvel could hear it. Her hands were all sweaty too. As she and Sadie bade him good night, she said, "I can't believe he really talked to me! He is such a fine, educated person. I was honored to have him speak to me." Hanna was so excited, she felt as though her feet weren't touching the ground.

"Hanna, maybe our fine, educated young man is interested in something more than your father's books. Hasn't he been coming to your house a lot lately?" Sadie asked.

"Yes," Hanna replied. "But since he never

really spoke to me, I didn't think he was interested in me. He seems to be so intense, so involved in everything. I hope to see him at other meetings."

When Hanna went to bed that night and closed her eyes, all she could see was Velvel's face: his big brown eyes, curly dark brown hair, jaunty mustache, and friendly smile.

10

The Big Question

Hanna and Velvel were sitting on a hill under a tree having a picnic. Hanna had brought Velvel to her favorite spot, her private place where she came to think. Years before, she had shared this place with Sadie, and now she brought Velvel here so they could have some time alone to get to know each other.

"These are good cookies, Hanna. Did you make them?" Velvel wiped away the sugar and crumbs clinging to his mustache. They had finished the butter and jelly sandwiches and dill pickles.

"I have been making these sugar cookies since I was ten years old," she laughed. "I am glad you like them." In the past few months since Velvel and

Hanna had been seeing each other at meetings, she had become less shy about speaking to him. She had found that he was very patient and kind in explaining things to her. She often asked him questions about the rights of the workers. He enjoyed long discussions. He also enjoyed helping people.

A breeze blew the basket over, and Hanna and Velvel both reached to catch it. It was a sunny summer day, very warm, but the breeze kept it from getting too hot. Hanna had on a new dress which she had just finished sewing. The fabric bloomed with pink and blue flowers, her favorite colors.

"Why are you looking at me?" Hanna shyly dropped her head when she realized Velvel was staring at her. She thought maybe something was wrong, that her hair was out of place or there was a spot on her dress.

"I never noticed how blue your eyes are," Velvel replied. Suddenly, he was shy too. The only times they had been together were at meetings with many other people around or at her house with all her family there.

There was a pause while they each wondered what to say next. Finally, Velvel asked, "Would you like to go to the next Zionist meeting with me on Sunday?"

"Yes, of course," Hanna replied. She had been to many meetings with Velvel over the past few months. Some of the meetings had been for the workers. Some meetings had been lectures. Sometimes young people from the wealthier families who had been away to universities would give talks on current events. This was of great interest to the people of Parichi. Since most of them did not travel, they did not know what was going on in the large cities of Russia. The Zionist meetings were organized to establish a Jewish homeland in Palestine. The hope was that Jews would finally have a place to live where they would not be persecuted.

"I shall come for you at two o'clock. The meeting will be in the usual place." Velvel started helping Hanna pack the basket. The "usual place" was an hour's walk into the woods near Parichi. Government officials would not give their permission for these meetings, so people met in a safe place, deep in the woods.

The meeting place was beautiful. The trees were so tall they blocked out the sun. Right in the middle of the forest was a clearing that seemed as though it was just waiting for them. The patches of light shining through the leaves and the large group gathering in silence gave the scene an eerie quality. There was always a sense of danger, a threat of being caught, but it was so exciting, not only to Hanna, but to all of the young people, that they gladly took the chance. These meetings brought light to their otherwise dull lives. They felt they had something to look forward to, something to live for.

That evening, as they walked home from the meeting, Hanna asked, "Do you think we shall ever really have a Jewish homeland?"

"As long as there are people like us who are willing to donate a *shekel* and work to support it, yes, I do," said Velvel. "I would go there now if it were possible."

"You would?" asked Hanna. "I don't know if I could leave my home and family to go to a strange land."

"What is so wonderful to keep us here in Russia?" he asked. "A life of hard work with nothing to show for it? And always the threat of being beaten, even murdered, simply because we are Jews?"

Hanna did not wish to see Velvel upset. She enjoyed his sense of humor, but also respected his serious side. Hanna did not think it was really so bad in Parichi. It was the only way of life she had ever known. She wondered what she would do if she left Parichi and things were even worse somewhere else.

As life went on, reports were given at meetings about terrible things happening in the cities of Russia. Laws had been laid down, keeping Jews away from their synagogues. Also, they were not allowed to own land, practice medicine or law, or hold public office. The strict laws stated that only a very few Jews were allowed to attend universities. Without an education, they were doomed to the same kind of life forever. They would never be allowed to better themselves.

It was another warm summer day. Hanna and Velvel were having a picnic at their favorite spot on the hill. They had finished eating, and were sitting on a cloth on the ground. Velvel had been teasing

56

her, and they had been laughing. Suddenly, Velvel became very serious.

"Hanna, I have something to tell you."

"What is it, Velvel?" she asked.

"I have been told to report for a physical examination. It will soon be time for me to serve in the Russian army."

"Oh no, oh no!" Hanna cried. She knew that very often Jewish boys were sent on the most dangerous missions. They seldom came home from the army alive. Hanna tried to be brave, but she couldn't keep the tears back. Velvel offered his handkerchief to dry her tears.

"Don't cry, Hanna. Things are not as bad as they seem. I have plans which will keep me out of the army," he said.

"You do?" she asked, as she wiped her eyes.

"You wouldn't think me a coward if I didn't want to serve in the army?" he asked.

"Oh no. I think you are a very brave person, Velvel."

"What you think is very important to me, Hanna," he said. "In fact, you have become the most important thing in my life. Whatever my future holds, I want to share it with you."

Hanna gasped. She wasn't sure she understood what he was saying.

Velvel smiled. "I am not saying this very well. This last year has been the most wonderful year of my life because of you. I don't want a day to go by when I can't see you smile or hear you laugh. What I am saying is, I love you. I want to marry you!"

Hanna's heart was beating so loudly, she just knew Velvel could hear it. "I love you too," she replied.

Velvel leaned over and kissed her gently. Hanna laughed.

He looked surprised. "What is so funny?"

"I am so happy!" she said. "And your mustache tickles!"

"Oh, Hanna, I can see that we shall have a very happy life together." He shook his head as he laughed with her.

On the walk home with her, Velvel said, "I must do the proper thing and ask your father for his permission to marry you. I know my father approves. I think he fell in love with you before I did, back when we were building the house and you brought water to us. He kept telling me what a sweet, shy girl you were and what a good daughter, so helpful to her mother."

"I am glad he approves of me. When do you want to ask Papa?" Hanna was swinging the basket as she walked.

"Tonight! I couldn't wait! I don't think you will be able to keep this secret either!" His eyes twinkled as he smiled at her.

"You are always teasing me! I could keep it a secret if I wanted to," she said with a toss of her head. "But I think it is a good idea to ask him tonight." Hanna's eyes sparkled with excitement.

That night Hanna and Mama sat in the parlor doing their needlework. The boys were reading. Velvel and Papa had been talking in the library for what seemed like hours to Hanna.

Finally, they came into the parlor and joined the rest of the family. Hanna looked from Papa to Velvel, but nothing showed in their faces. She suddenly had a feeling of panic. What if Papa said no? What if Velvel changed his mind?

"It is getting late," said Papa. "Boys, it is time for bed. Mama and I shall retire too. Hanna, you may talk to Velvel for a few minutes before he leaves."

"Good night," they all said. The boys put away their books, and Mama put away her sewing. Everyone left. Suddenly, the room was very quiet.

Velvel sat down gently next to Hanna. "Your father and I have had a long discussion. He is very concerned about your future and your happiness. I admire him very much. I hope that someday I can be the same kind of father to our children."

"Does that mean that he gave his permission for us to marry?" Hanna asked.

"Yes," Velvel replied. "But before you make your final decision, there are some things we need to talk about."

Hanna sat quietly with her hands in her lap. "Then let's talk," she said.

"We have gotten to know each other pretty well these past months. I have found it easy to talk to you. We have gone to many meetings and shared our ideas about the workers in the factories, about the events going on in Russia and about the need for a Jewish homeland. Now we need to talk about the possibility of emigrating, of leaving Russia. I have come to believe that we Jews have no future here. We are young. You are almost eighteen and I am almost twenty. There is much I want to do with my life. I want our children to grow up free, with no limits set on their lives. What I want to know is, how do you feel about leaving Russia and starting a new life with me somewhere else?"

Hanna was stunned. There was a moment of silence while she gathered her thoughts together. "I don't know what to say. I love you and want to marry you. But I don't know if I can leave my family, my friends. This may not be perfect, but it is my home. Where would we go? What would we do? How would we live?"

Velvel took Hanna's hands in his and said, "As long as we love each other, we shall work it out. All I know is that here nothing changes for the better. Things only get worse for us. I want the best for my family. I want you to think about it; we will talk again tomorrow."

With that he kissed her cheek, got up, and quietly slipped out the door into the night.

11

The Engagement

The next day, there was much to talk about at the Gorelik house. Hanna was surprised at her brothers' reaction to the news. Haskell and Morris very tenderly told her they loved her and hoped she would be happy. It made her cry. She suddenly realized her little brothers were growing up to be sensitive young men. David even hugged her. He was excited about the possibility of attending his first wedding. There was a time, not too long ago, when Hanna could have gladly given them all away. They were always bothering her. She remembered all the times she had to babysit with them. Now only David still needed watching.

"I think he is a fine young man," said Mama.

"But why does he need to take you away? He could continue working for his father, and you both could live with us."

"Mama, he wants to be more than a carpenter. He wants to use his mind instead of his hands. He dreams of building a business of his own. How can he do that here? What kind of future would we have with the six rubles a week he earns from his father?" Hanna said.

"It sounds as if you have made up your mind, my daughter," said Papa.

"We have many things to decide. But I do love him. He says we can work everything out," said Hanna.

"He told me he is being called into the army soon," said Papa.

"That is true. Velvel said he has planned a way to get out of it, but I don't know how he can."

"Could you be happy living away from us? Who knows where he will take you? We might never see you again." Mama was making no attempt to hide her tears. Hanna had always held a special place in Mama's heart, being the oldest child and the only girl.

"Oh, Mama, it is so hard being an adult. I wish I could go back to being a little girl. All I had to worry about were my lessons." Hanna threw herself into Mama's arms, and they cried together.

"Maybe I should just tell him no," said Papa.

"No, Papa. Please let me make this decision myself. We shall talk again tonight. He really wants what is best for me too," Hanna told him.

"All right, if it will make you happy." Papa hugged Hanna. "All we want is for you to be happy."

"I know, and I love you both." Hanna kissed Mama and Papa. "I need to spend some time by myself now. My sewing will have to wait. I shall do it later." Hanna slowly walked to her special place on the hill. She had a lot of thinking to do.

Later that evening, as the sun was going down, there was a knock at the door. Hanna ran to the door and opened it. It was Velvel. He had a look of pain on his face. He was limping as he hobbled into the room. He tried to smile as he greeted everyone, then fell into the nearest chair.

"Velvel, what has happened? Why are you limping?" asked Hanna.

"Do you remember I told you I would find a way to stay out of the czar's army?" he asked Hanna.

"Yes, I remember. Velvel, what have you done?" Hanna asked.

"I won't be going into the army now. I have cut off my big toe." Velvel looked at Hanna out of the corner of his eye to see how she was taking the news.

"Oh my God!" Hanna exclaimed. "Will you be all right?"

"I shall be fine in no time. I am not the first Jewish man to do this. With shoes on, who is going to notice I only have nine toes?" He tried again to smile at his joke, but it was hard because he was in pain.

As they talked on through the evening, Velvel told them he heard there was going to be a meeting to help people immigrate to America.

"I think we should go and hear what they have to say," Velvel said, looking at Hanna.

"Yes, we shall go to the meeting," Hanna agreed. "Meanwhile, shall we start making plans for our wedding?"

"Yes," said Velvel, giving her a hug. "The sooner the better. I don't want you to have a chance to change your mind!"

Mama and Papa laughed. "I don't think you need to worry about that. Once Hanna makes up her mind about something, that is it! You will find out very soon," Papa told him. They all laughed.

Hanna and Velvel decided to wait a year to marry. They needed time to save their money. They would still have to live with their parents until they had enough saved for their own home.

"We need to let everyone know the wonderful news. We shall have an engagement party. We shall invite all our relatives. They will want to meet you, Velvel," Mama said.

"That is a lovely idea," Hanna said as she looked at Velvel. He nodded his approval of the idea.

The next week was taken up with plans for the party. Hanna and Mama wrote letters to *Bubbye* and all the other relatives. *Zayde* had died last year. Hanna was sad when she thought how much he would have enjoyed seeing her married. He had often teased her about growing up and getting married. But there was so much to do, she didn't dwell on that subject.

The house was cleaned as it had never been cleaned before. The boys carried the mattresses outside to air. Then they took all the rugs outside and beat them until there was not a speck of dust left on them. Hanna heard them grumbling among themselves about all the work they had to do. "Wouldn't it be a lot less trouble if Hanna and Velvel just run off to get married?" Hanna smiled to herself when she heard the boys muttering. She knew her brothers were really excited for her. It was just their way to complain about all the work.

"Hanna, I found something that has been stored away for many years. You may wear it if you want to. Here, try it on." Mama handed Hanna an old box. Hanna opened it and pulled out a wedding dress, somewhat yellowed with age.

"Mama, look! It is still beautiful. I had forgotten about your dress. You used to take it out sometimes and let me look at it. Even the lace is still in good condition." Hanna held the dress up to herself and twirled around the room. "It looks like it will fit. I hope so. I would love to wear it."

"Why don't I freshen it up? Then you can try it on. While I am doing that, you can take down the curtains, and we shall wash them too." Mama told her.

Mama carefully washed and ironed the dress.

65

She brought it to Hanna and helped her put it on. After she finished buttoning all the tiny buttons, Mama stepped back and looked at Hanna.

"My, if I don't feel like I am looking in a mirror! You look just like I did when I was your age." Mama shook her head and sat down to gaze at Hanna in the wedding dress.

"Mama, we are exactly the same size. It won't even need to be altered," said Hanna. "I wonder where I can find a piece of lace for a veil?"

"We will have plenty of time to send for some lace," said Mama. "You haven't even set a date yet for the wedding."

Hanna took the dress off. She carefully folded it back into the box, wrapping it in clean cloth to protect it. Then she slid the box under her bed.

The day of the party arrived. All the windows sparkled. The rugs and curtains were back in place. Everything was scrubbed clean. *Bubbye* arrived early to help with the party. She hugged Hanna tightly.

"When I look at you, I remember a little girl with braided hair and ribbons. What happened to her?" *Bubbye* asked.

"She grew up. I mean, I grew up," laughed Hanna.

"You certainly did, into a lovely young lady," *Bubbye* said and hugged her again.

As the rest of the relatives assembled that evening, many of them said the same thing to Hanna. Some had not seen her in a long time. Most people didn't travel. They worked all week and rested on the Sabbath. The only time to travel was for weddings and funerals and holidays.

Hanna enjoyed greeting her aunts, uncles, and cousins. She nervously introduced them to Velvel. She wanted them to like him. But she need not have worried. He was liked by everyone. He was naturally friendly and knew how to joke with them and make them laugh. Hanna also enjoyed visiting with Velvel's parents and his sisters, Esther and Dora, and his brother, Sol. Mr. Astonovitsky was very happy with the idea of having Hanna as his daughter-in-law. He told Papa that they were the perfect match, a match made in heaven!

Everyone raised their glasses, while Papa chanted a blessing. Then he toasted the couple, saying, "To Hanna, my daughter, and to Velvel, soon to be my son-in-law. May you have many years of happiness together."

They all clinked their glasses together. Then everyone ate the refreshments of herring and small slices of rye bread. When all the food and wine were gone, everyone went home.

12

The Meeting

Velvel came to take Hanna to the immigration meeting. Morris and Haskell decided to go with them. Haskell had just started working as an iron worker in a factory that made anchors for ships. Mama and Papa weren't happy with his decision to work in the factory. They wanted him to continue his studies and become a Hebrew teacher. He was a smart boy, but he was tired of bending over his books, never getting much fresh air. Even though the work was hard, he enjoyed earning his own money.

Morris had gone to work as an apprentice for a tailor. He was learning how to sew men's clothing. He agreed to work for a year with no pay to learn the work. After that, he would be paid very little to start out, but he hoped that with time he would be able to earn a living. David was still in *cheder,* with no plans yet for his future.

Many people gathered for the meeting that night. The leader of the meeting was a Jew from Minsk, Hyman Rabinowitz. He had been contacted by a Jewish organization in America to help people immigrate.

Someone in the gathering asked, "Is it true that in America the streets are paved with gold?"

Some of the group laughed. Mr. Rabinowitz replied, "There is no gold lying on the streets. However, if you are willing to work hard, you will be able to earn all the money you need to live a comfortable life."

Mr. Rabinowitz started to tell the crowd what it was like in America. So many people were crowding into New York City that living conditions were very bad.

"I am sure you have friends who have gone to live in America. How many here know people who have immigrated to America?" Mr. Rabinowitz asked. Many people raised their hands. "How many here know people who live in New York?" he asked the group. The same group of people raised their hands again.

"Why have they not moved to other cities, if it is so crowded there?" Haskell asked.

"They want to stay with their own people. They want to have someone with whom they can speak

Russian and Yiddish. But it has put a terrible strain on our people to find places to live. Sometimes two or three families live together in a small apartment. This also makes it hard to find good jobs. Some people sell from pushcarts in the street. Many people work in the garment business. They sew in their homes or in large factories," Mr. Rabinowitz told them.

"You told us before we could earn all the money we needed for a comfortable life. Now you tell us how bad things are in New York. Why would we want to go there?" asked Morris.

"That is a good question, young man," said Mr. Rabinowitz. "The answer is we have made plans to send people, not to New York, but to Galveston, Texas."

"Texas . . . I have heard of it," someone said. "There are savage Indians there who will kill you." Suddenly, everyone began talking at once.

Mr. Rabinowitz held out his hands to get order. "That is no longer a problem. What we have to offer you is a new start in life. We have people in several states who will sponsor you and give you jobs. They will help you find places to live. This way, you won't be crowded together in one city. There is plenty of room for you. You will be spread out across many towns and states."

"How do we keep our religion with no other Jews around?" someone asked.

"You will be sent to cities and towns where Jews

are already living. It won't be easy, but it can be done," Mr. Rabinowitz answered.

"Where do we sail from? How much does it cost? How long is the trip?" The questions were coming from all over the room.

"Quiet, please. I will be glad to answer all your questions." Mr. Rabinowitz continued. "We sail from Bremen, Germany. The trip takes three weeks. You will need fifty rubles for the trip, plus a little money to get you started. If you are wondering why, after all these years, an immigration port opened in Galveston, I shall tell you. A very wealthy Jew, Jacob Schiff from New York, saw the problem of Jewish immigration and the crowded conditions on New York's Lower East Side. He decided to do something about it. He organized the Jewish Immigration Society to help you come to America. Please take one of these leaflets, which should answer all your questions. There is information here on who to contact, if you are interested."

As he passed out the leaflets, Mr. Rabinowitz said, "I can't promise you much, but you will have a better life in America than you have now. There will be no one telling you how to live or what to believe. You will be able to practice your religion without fear. So, you decide. It is up to you."

Velvel took a leaflet and looked at Hanna. "This is it. This is our future." He picked Hanna up and swung her around. Hanna nodded yes. She couldn't speak. There was a lump in her throat and tears in her eyes.

13

The Wedding

"If America is half as good as Mr. Rabinowitz said, I am ready to go," Haskell told Morris.

"Let's go!" said Morris. "We could all go together." The Gorelik family were all sitting around the table discussing the meeting. It was all they had talked about since the meeting the night before.

"You are all ready to go to a strange country after only one meeting? You are getting carried away with this idea of immigrating to America." Papa was upset. He had always made the decisions for the family. Now his children were growing up. He felt like he was losing control of the family. He feared the children might be jumping into something they knew nothing about.

"Are you ready to split up the family?" Papa

asked of them. He looked from Haskell to Morris to Hanna. "Mama and David and I shall be here and you will be thousands of miles away. We might never see each other again."

"Oh, Papa, don't say that," Hanna pleaded. "Several people told us how whole families immigrate. First, one member goes. He works and saves his money. He sends it home to his family. Then they are able to join him. We could do it . . . I know we could. If we all work hard and save our money, it could happen."

"How many years would that take? We would be old. We might not want to move to a new place, leave our friends, learn a new language." Mama was upset too. She was used to her life in Parichi. She had never thought about moving to another town, much less another country.

"Have you thought about how you would leave the country?" Papa asked. "The czar will not allow people to come and go as they please."

"We met people at the meeting who know how to obtain papers to get across the border. With a few rubles for the security guards, one can get out of the country easily," Hanna told them.

"What about your wedding? We have a lot to do. When do you plan to get married?" Mama asked.

"Velvel and I want to be married next month," Hanna said. "I know we had planned to wait a year to marry, but everything has changed. If Velvel can get enough money together for one ticket, then he will go as soon as possible. I shall join him later."

"Why don't you both work and save your money? Then you can travel together," Papa said.

"We would like to travel together," Hanna said. "But it would take much longer to save the money here. If Velvel could send American dollars, they are worth twice as much as rubles."

"So you plan to marry and then be separated for who knows how long? How do you feel about that?" Mama asked.

"I am not happy about being separated, but we will write letters, lots of letters. We shall be working hard, and the time will pass fast. I shall need you to help me get through it." Hanna held out her hands to Mama and Papa. They all joined hands around the table and said a silent prayer.

"Then, if it is all decided, we have a wedding to plan." Mama put a smile on her face as she wiped away a tear.

During the next few weeks, Hanna was so busy she hardly had time to get her sewing done. Mrs. Chernov had sent some sewing to Hanna. When she stopped by to pick it up, she was surprised that Hanna didn't have it finished. Hanna was always so good about having things done on time. Even as a little girl, Hanna had been a serious student. She always finished her assignments on time.

"Mrs. Chernov, I am so sorry the dress isn't ready. I shall have it finished tomorrow and bring it to you." Hanna went to her room to finish sewing the dress.

"Mrs. Chernov, sit down and have some coffee," said Mama. Mrs. Chernov sat down, while Mama got coffee for both of them. Mama joined her at the table. "Did you know that Hanna and Velvel are getting married in two weeks?" she asked.

74

"No," said Mrs. Chernov. "I didn't know they were getting married that soon. No wonder Hanna didn't have time to finish my sewing."

"This has all come up since the immigration meeting. Hanna and Velvel have their hearts set on going to America . . . Haskell and Morris too. They have all started working until very late at night to earn the money to go," Mama told her.

"What can I do to help?" asked Mrs. Chernov.

"Hanna plans to wear my wedding dress, but she needs a veil. We were going to order some lace, but I am afraid it won't get here in time. Do you know where we can find some pretty lace?" Mama asked.

"I put some away a few years ago when I made a wedding dress for my niece. I shall see if it is what Hanna wants. If she likes it, it will be my pleasure to give it to her," said Mrs. Chernov.

"That is very nice of you. But we would be happy to give you something for it," Mama said.

"Hanna has always held a special place in my heart. I want to do something nice for her. I still remember the first time she came for a sewing lesson. Her basket was brimming over, and her eyes were big and full of wonder. I am proud of her. She sews as well as I do now — better on some things," laughed Mrs. Chernov.

Mama didn't tell Hanna about her talk with Mrs. Chernov. Mama wanted to keep the lace a surprise. She also didn't want Hanna to be disappointed if the lace was unsuitable.

Velvel came to see Hanna almost every evening. He was working on a house nearby, so he stopped on his way home. Sometimes he was so tired, he almost fell asleep as they sat talking. When she saw he was about to nod off, she would send him home to sleep.

One night, as they made plans for the wedding, Velvel said, "We have just the right amount of brothers. With your three brothers and my brother, each can hold a corner of the *chuppa* at the wedding."

"Do you think David is tall enough to hold one of the corner poles?" Hanna asked. "I would hate for the *chuppa* to come crashing down on our heads!"

Velvel laughed. "You may still think of David as a little child, but he is growing up. We can get someone to help him. We don't want him to feel left out."

"You are right. I just don't want anything to go wrong," Hanna said. "There is a great deal to think about. I am helping Sadie sew her bridesmaid's dress. Mama needs my help in making her dress too. I am the only one not getting a new dress," she suddenly realized.

"What old rag will you be wearing?" asked Velvel with a smile.

"I can't tell you. It isn't proper for the groom to see the dress ahead of time. So I must not tell you about it either."

"I have always liked surprises," said Velvel, "especially if they are good surprises. My favorite times are birthdays and *Chanukah,* when we can find surprises in little packages."

"There will be plenty of surprises for you at our wedding, all good ones." Hanna was thinking of the band of musicians Papa had hired. Velvel loved music. He always whistled as he came to the house, no matter how tired he was. Hanna knew Velvel would enjoy the music.

"I look forward to all the wonderful surprises. It is getting late now, and I must go. We both need our rest," said Velvel. Hanna walked him to the door. He hugged her and was gone.

The next two weeks passed in a blur. Hanna wished for a quiet time to sit under her tree and dream, but there was too much to do. Velvel's mother and sisters wanted Hanna's approval on their new dresses. They had several meetings together. Hanna helped them put the finishing touches on their dresses.

Morris was a big help. He did the tailoring of the groom's new suit. He altered all the other men's suits. The young men were still growing. They couldn't afford new suits, so the old ones had to be made to fit.

The day of the wedding arrived, bright and sunny. Relatives and friends from out of town made their way to the Gorelik house. As sundown approached, everyone had changed into their wedding clothes. All the men had polished their shoes until they shined like new. Mama looked like a young girl herself in her new dress of pink with a lace collar. But there was nothing to compare with the beauty of the bride.

Hanna had often dreamed about her wedding day. As little girls, she and Sadie would play "wedding" with their paper dolls. They would use a little piece of cloth with four sticks attached to the corners. The dolls would stand under the *chuppa*, while Hanna and Sadie got them married.

As Hanna looked at herself in the mirror, Mama placed the wedding veil on her head. Mrs. Chernov had brought it to Hanna, saying, "This is my wedding gift to you. I hope you like it."

"It is beautiful. Thank you, Mrs. Chernov." Hanna hugged her. She thought to herself what a dear teacher and friend she had.

Hanna's reflection looked back at her from the mirror. Mama asked, "What are you thinking on your wedding day? You are very quiet."

Hanna smiled. "I was just wondering who that person in the mirror is. It couldn't be me. I have never looked like this before. I don't feel old enough to be a bride. Sometimes I don't feel any different than when I was twelve years old."

"That is because you are still the same sweet person you have always been, but more grown up. After all, you are almost eighteen," Mama reminded her.

"Is this my little Hanna?" *Bubbye* gasped as she entered the room. She took in the sight of Hanna in her wedding dress. "You look just like your mother did in that dress. She was a beautiful bride too."

"Thank you, *Bubbye*," said Hanna.

"Are you dressed yet?" Sadie called.

"Yes, come in Sadie." Hanna turned to face her as Sadie stood in the doorway. "Well, say something," Hanna said.

"You just took my breath away. You are a lovely bride," she said softly.

"Oh, Sadie, I'm a bride . . . I'm a bride . . . I'm a bride!"

Sadie grabbed her hands, and they twirled each other around the room chanting, "I'm a bride . . . I'm a bride . . . I'm a bride!"

Mama and *Bubbye* scooted out the door to give them more room. They stood in the doorway, watching and laughing.

Mama suddenly remembered the time. "Hanna, it is time to go. You don't want to be late to your own wedding!"

Hanna, with her parents on both sides of her, started walking down the street to the synagogue. They were followed by her brothers, *Bubbye,* Sadie, and all the other relatives and friends who had been gathering all day.

At the synagogue, Hanna saw a large group of people. The crowd parted to allow her to walk up the steps of the synagogue to the *chuppa.*

It is indeed beautiful, she thought. It was decorated with flowers on top. Greenery wound its way down the poles, making it seem like it had grown there. Her brothers took their places at the corners of the *chuppa* to hold the poles. David proudly held his pole with only a little help from a neighbor.

Already standing under the *chuppa* was the rabbi, the *chazzan,* and Velvel with his parents. Sol was holding one of the poles. Esther and Dora were standing behind their parents. Nearby stood a choir of men from the synagogue. They sang a hymn as Hanna took her place under the *chuppa.* She looked at Velvel. She had never seen him look more handsome.

The ceremony started. The rabbi explained the duties of husband and wife. He blessed the wine, and the *chazzan* sang the blessings. His voice floated out over the crowd of people. Hanna and Velvel each took a sip of wine from the same glass. Velvel slipped a plain gold band on Hanna's finger. When the ceremony was over, a glass was placed on the floor. Velvel lifted his foot and brought it down hard, smashing the glass into tiny pieces. This was a reminder of the destruction of the holy Temple in Jerusalem.

As the glass shattered, everyone shouted, *"Mazel tov! Mazel tov!"* The musicians struck up a lively song. Hanna and Velvel led the wedding party through the streets to the Goreliks' house. *Bubbye* was one of the guests who danced all the way from the synagogue to the house.

Velvel turned to Hanna. "Is the band one of the surprises?"

"Yes. Do you like them?" Hanna asked.

"Yes! I look forward to a lifetime of surprises with you." With that, he lifted Hanna off the ground, and twirled her around and around as the guests applauded.

14

Goodbye, Velvel

People were everywhere. The furniture had been pushed back to make room for tables and chairs. There was plenty to eat and drink. Everyone was talking and laughing. It was very noisy, but the neighbors didn't mind. They were there too. It seemed like the whole town turned out for the wedding. There was no way Mama could cook for this many people; all the neighbors brought food. The tables groaned under the weight of all the sweet cookies and cakes.

Hanna and Velvel received many useful gifts to start their life together. His parents gave them a huge brass samovar. Her parents gave them a feather bed and two large feather pillows. *Bubbye* gave them linens which she made herself. She embroidered each pillowcase with flowers. Hanna still had the pillowcases she had made when she first learned to sew. She was glad now she had made them.

Velvel gave her a dainty locket. Hanna put both their pictures in it. She gave Velvel a watch. He was very pleased with it. He checked it every few minutes just so he could look at it. Their friends gave them a pair of tall candlesticks. Hanna was very happy with all the gifts. She thought, *Now we have everything we need to start our life together.*

The tables and chairs were pushed back so that the dancing could begin. The men did the traditional folk dances together. It wasn't considered proper for men and women to dance together. After the men finished their dancing, the women got into a circle and danced around Hanna.

When the song ended, two chairs were brought to the center of the room. Hanna sat in one chair and Velvel in the other. The men formed a circle around Velvel and the women around Hanna. All of a sudden, Hanna and Velvel found themselves high in the air. The lively dance started. Some of the stronger young people raised the chairs and swayed to the music. The rest of the dancers circled around them. Hanna was laughing so hard, she almost fell out of the chair.

"Don't drop me," she pleaded.

"We won't." Sadie laughed, looking up at her.

Hanna's new sisters-in-law were helping hold her up too.

It was very late before the music stopped and everyone went to sleep. The out-of-town relatives spent the night. There were beds of blankets on the floor of every room.

The next day was *Shabbos*. They all went together to the synagogue. The rabbi said a special prayer for the happiness of the bride and groom. Afterwards, everyone came back to the house to eat. That night, the musicians returned. The house was again filled with music. The dancing went on all night.

After the weekend filled with wedding celebrations, Hanna and Velvel settled into their day-to-day activities. They decided to live with the Goreliks for a while. Hanna took up her sewing, and Velvel continued to work for his father.

One evening several months later, Velvel rushed in. His voice was filled with excitement. "They came. The papers came!"

"What papers?" Hanna asked.

"The papers which allow me to cross the border from Russia into Germany." He had already received his emigration papers.

"What is wrong, Hanna?" Velvel noticed a tear sliding down her cheek.

Hanna quickly brushed the tear away. "Nothing. It is just that we have waited so long. Now that it is time, I don't want you to go."

"You can't mean that. We have talked a lot

about America. I have worked hard to get all the papers. We agreed it is the place for us to go." He looked at her, puzzled.

"I know. I am just scared," Hanna said softly.

"Scared of what?" he asked.

"Scared of having you go far away from me. Scared that something might happen, and we might never see each other again." By now, Hanna was crying. Velvel put his arms around her. He patted her like her mother used to when she was scared of the dark.

"I know. I know. Don't you think I am scared too? I can't speak English. I don't know how long it will take to save the money to send for you. But you can be sure of one thing. I will send every dollar I can spare until I have you with me." Velvel looked into her eyes.

"I know," Hanna replied.

"We must be strong. This is what is best for us. I just know it," Velvel told her.

"When you talk to me, I know it too. I shall try to be strong while you are away," Hanna said.

News traveled fast in Parichi. Before long, meetings were being held by the young men who would be traveling together. Several men would be on the next ship sailing from Bremen, Germany, to Galveston, Texas. Velvel would be one of them.

Velvel decided to take only his clothes tied up in a bundle. He would be renting a room and wouldn't need anything else. When Hanna came, she would bring their household goods.

85

It was a cold winter day. Velvel stood in his warmest clothes, saying goodbye to Hanna and both their families.

"Don't forget to stay bundled up," his mother told him.

"Take care of yourself," his father said.

"Don't forget to write us," Mama and Papa said.

"I love you," Hanna told him. "I will write every day."

"I love you too," Velvel said. "Take care of each other. I shall be fine," he told them all.

He and the other men climbed aboard a horse-drawn wagon after they had tossed their bundles in the back. The wagon would take them as far as the border. Someone would be waiting on the other side to transport them the rest of the way.

Hanna couldn't help the tears that came, but she stood tall and proud and waved until the wagon was out of sight. Then she turned and walked back into the house.

"The time will pass fast," Mama said.

"You will be together again before you know it," Papa said.

Hanna knew they were trying to make her feel better. But at that moment she felt awfully lonely.

15

Letters From America

At first, the days seemed to drag by. Then Hanna became so busy sewing she had to hire another girl to help her. Always at night, in her bed, she got out paper and pen and wrote to Velvel. She told him everything that happened that day and always tried to remember something funny to tell him. She liked to think of him laughing as he read her letters. In one letter, she wrote:

> David was helping Mama by delivering some food to a sick neighbor. I watched at the window as he struggled through the snow. The packages were very heavy. More snow fell last night, and it was very deep. I was just about to turn away from the window when he fell. He didn't just plop down. He tripped over something buried deep in the

snow. The packages went flying out of his hands. He was sprawled out face down in the snow. I shouted to Mama to come look. We both stood at the window and laughed until tears ran down our faces. David was so angry, he got up and kicked at the snow. Finally, we put on our coats and went out to help him pick up the packages. They weren't harmed since they fell in the soft snow. We put them in his arms and sent him on his way. He is usually very good about helping. But when things don't go his way, he shows his temper!

It had been over three weeks, and Hanna was thinking to herself that Velvel should have arrived in Texas by now. The mail came, and there was a letter from Velvel. It was the first letter she ever received from America. Hanna was very excited. She carefully opened the envelope. There was Velvel's familiar, strong handwriting.

My dearest Hanna,

I am writing to you from Fort Worth, Texas. Mr. Rosenthal, who owns a meat packing plant, has very kindly given me a job. It is hard work, but I am glad to do it. I carry the sides of beef from the ice box to the wagons, which then deliver the meat to stores.

I am living with Max and Rosa Katzenbaum. They are related to Sadie's family. I am renting their extra bedroom. It is for their baby daughter. But for now their daughter sleeps in their bedroom. For the present I have my own room.

The name of the ship I sailed on was the *Chemnitz*. It is a huge ship. The trip was very long. I don't think I shall go on another voyage across the water for a long time! I ate the herring and bread you sent with me. I was lucky not to get sick. Many passengers did. Most of the trip was smooth, although we did have a few days of bad weather. But I don't wish to talk about the trip anymore. It is behind me and now I move on.

I became friends with several men on the ship who also came to Fort Worth. There is a large group of Jews in this city. They are kind to newcomers, but they also tease us and call us "greenhorns."

When I got off the ship, people were selling fruit from carts. I stopped to look it over. I bought a long yellow fruit. I bit into it, and it tasted terrible! My new friends laughed at me as I spit it out. They pointed to a man standing nearby who was eating the same kind of fruit. He had peeled it and ate only the soft white inside. It is called a banana. I tried it again, this time peeling it. The inside is very good!

How are you, my dearest? Is your sewing keeping you busy? And how are your parents? And brothers? Please give them my best. And for you, I send my love,

Your husband,
Velvel

Hanna read the letter over and over until she knew it by memory. She tried to read between the lines. Maybe he didn't tell her everything. Maybe he was sick on the ship. Maybe the work is too hard for him. She read the letter to her family that evening.

"It is a good letter, Hanna," said Papa. "It sounds like he is doing fine. You must not read all your fears into his letters. Just read them and be happy that he is doing well."

"You are right, Papa. It is just that I can't help worrying about him."

The days went by. The letters came almost every day. Once a week, he sent money in his letters. One day, he wrote this to her:

My dearest Hanna,

I hope you and your family are well. I am working hard, as usual. Three nights a week I go to English classes. The Katzenbaums have been here two years and know the language. They are helping me learn to speak English. I shall help you when you get here. It is not very hard.

Times are not good here. Many banks are closed, and people are out of work. I am lucky to have a good job and be able to send money to you. After you get here, we shall save for our own business. Max and I have been talking about selling bananas. This is why I came, to find a way to make something of myself, to provide a good living for my family.

I hope it will not be too much longer until you can join me. I send my love.

Your husband,
Velvel

Hanna hugged the letter tightly. "I hope it won't be long, my husband, until I can see you too."

16

Last Days at Home

Almost a year had passed since Velvel left. He had been very good about writing to Hanna. She was learning a lot about America through his letters. He told her how kind people were, how they helped him learn English. He was learning more English words every day. He described Fort Worth for her:

It is a town whose main industry is cattle. People bring their cows here from all over the state. I have never seen so many cows together in one place. And the noise! When the pens are full at the stockyards, you can't imagine how loud it gets. The cows and their calves bawl for each other twenty-four hours a day. And the smell! When the wind is blowing, you can smell the cows for miles.

In another letter he told her:

It is much warmer here. The winters are not nearly as cold as in Russia, which is nice. But the summers get much hotter than we are used to. There are not nearly as many trees here. I missed our Russian forests, at first. But now I am used to it, and I like it. I hope you will like it too.

Hanna always shared his letters with Mama and Papa and the boys. She would read them aloud, all but the personal parts. One evening, they discussed Velvel and others they knew who were in America.

"Mrs. Brodsky told me her sister has been waiting six months for a letter from her husband," Mama told them. "You are lucky to have a husband who writes and sends money."

"Maybe Mrs. Brodsky's brother-in-law has had a hard time finding work. Maybe he is embarrassed to write when he can't send money," Hanna said.

"That is what I told her," Mama replied. "She is afraid something has happened to him." They all shook their heads, wondering why he had not written.

Most of the men who had emigrated from Russia wrote often. Many had settled in Texas. A few went on to Oklahoma, Kansas, and Missouri. Wives and daughters of these men shared their letters with each other. It helped to have friends who were going through the same thing. When a letter arrived from America, it was a time for rejoicing and sharing.

Velvel wrote that he was doing well. He still lived with the Katzenbaums and worked at the meat-packing plant. Hanna was overjoyed when his letters came. If money fell out when she opened them, it was an added joy, because she knew she was that much closer to seeing him again.

Hanna had been sewing until late every evening. Haskell and Morris worked hard too. Morris had just started earning money after working for a year as a tailor with no pay. Haskell and Hanna had almost enough money saved for their fares. On Hanna's eighteenth birthday, she had asked for no gifts. She only wanted money to get to America. It was a very lonely birthday without Velvel. Mama and Papa made it a real party, hoping that she wouldn't miss Velvel so much. They thought it might be the last birthday they would all be together.

"Mrs. Brodsky also told me that some of the men were unhappy in Texas. After a few months there, they moved to New York, where they have friends and relatives to help them," Mama said.

"Velvel is happy in Texas. He doesn't want to move to New York." Hanna was getting used to the idea of living in Texas. It was easier to picture herself living there than in a large eastern city like New York. She had lived all her life in a small town where everybody knew everyone else. She liked the fact that people cared about each other. There was always someone to help if help was needed.

Haskell and Morris were always talking about America. One evening, they came flying in the house.

"We just found out there is still room on the next ship to Galveston," said Haskell.

"I wish I had the money. I would leave right now," said Morris. "I hate this waiting. It is going to be another year before I have enough saved for a ticket." Morris was running out of patience.

"Velvel says the immigration officials are getting stricter," Hanna said. "If someone is ill or their papers are not in perfect order, they are sent back. Can you imagine saving for such a long time, traveling across the ocean, and then being sent back? He wants us to come as soon as possible."

"How can we get the money together any faster?" asked Haskell. "We are all working long hours now."

"I could sell my sewing machine!" said Hanna.

"But then how will you earn a living?" asked Mama.

"When we get to America, we shall save and buy another one. It would be hard to carry on the ship anyway. I don't know why I didn't think of it before."

"Do you know someone who could buy it?" asked Papa.

"Yes. Mrs. Chernov has some new pupils. They need good sewing machines. I shall ask her tomorrow if one of them might want to buy my machine."

"Tomorrow I shall see what papers we need," said Haskell.

"I shall write Velvel and tell him to get ready for us. He will need to find jobs for you," she told her brothers, "and he will find a place for us to live."

They were all so excited, they found it hard to go to sleep that night. Mama and Papa couldn't sleep either. They both thought about how quiet it would be with three of their children gone. They would miss them very much.

The next few weeks found the Goreliks in a flurry of activity. Hanna was able to sell her sewing machine to a student of Mrs. Chernov. When Hanna's parents and Velvel's parents saw they only needed a few more rubles, they gave the young people their savings.

At a family meeting in the Goreliks' kitchen, the Astonovitskys presented Hanna with the money she and her brothers needed for the trip.

"We don't need much to live on. We want you and your brothers to have a new start in life."

Hanna threw her arms around them. With tears in her eyes, she said, "We don't know how to thank you. With this money and the money my parents have given us, we shall be able to take the next ship to America."

Haskell and Morris could no longer hold their excitement. They stood up and cheered, then danced around the room. Within moments, they had everyone singing and dancing, laughing and crying at the same time.

Haskell got all their papers in order. He made arrangements for them to travel by wagon to Minsk. Then they would take a train to Bremen. Hanna wrote Velvel to tell him of their plans. He wrote back:

> I am very happy that you will be here soon. I am counting the days until I see your face again. Haskell and Morris will have work. They can help me in my produce business. By the time you arrive, Max and I should be ready to start our business. We have almost enough saved for a pushcart. We have also located a place to buy fruit and

vegetables. What do you think about this? Your husband will be an American businessman! As soon as you get here, we shall apply for American citizenship. What do you think of that?

As Hanna read his letter, she could feel the excitement flowing from Velvel's words. All that he had dreamed was going to come true. She just knew it!

The day finally arrived for their departure. It was a cold, dreary December day. The grayness of the day seemed to affect them. Even though Hanna felt excited and a little scared about the long ocean trip, she also felt sad knowing she would never see her home again.

"Are you sure you have everything?" Mama looked at the huge bundle as Hanna tied it in a tight knot.

"If there was anything else, I don't know how we would carry it!"

Haskell and Morris had only a few clothes to carry. They would help Hanna by carrying all her household goods.

"I have all our wedding gifts and my clothes. I didn't know we had so much until I tried to pick it up," Hanna laughed. She tried to make a joke to cheer Mama up.

"Do you promise to write every week?" Mama asked.

"Yes, Mama. I promise," said Hanna.

"Will you tell us the good and the bad? Don't protect us."

"Yes, Mama. I shall tell you everything. You will share our lives, even though we are far apart."

"Good," said Mama.

"Now, will you do something for me?" asked Hanna.

"What is that, Hanna?"

"Will you and Papa think about coming to America?"

There was a moment of silence. "Yes, we shall think about it," Mama said softly.

As Mama and Hanna hugged each other and cried, Haskell and Morris called to them.

"Are you ready?" Haskell called.

"It is time to go!" Morris shouted.

"Yes, I am ready. Come! Get my things!" Hanna called to them.

The brothers loaded everything into the waiting wagon. There were several people they knew already on the wagon. They kissed Mama, Papa, David, and the Astonovitskys goodbye. They climbed aboard, and the wagon began its journey.

Hanna looked back, trying to memorize every house, every tree. She waved until she could no longer see her family. Then she turned around and said to herself, "Goodbye, Mama. Goodbye, Papa. I know we shall see each other again someday."

17

America at Last

When they arrived in Minsk, the wagon took them directly to the train station. After everyone was aboard the train, an official came through checking the tickets and passports. Hanna was very nervous. What if their papers weren't in order? What if they were put off the train? But all the official did was look at the papers, return them, and go on to the next person.

Hanna pulled out some herring and dark bread and passed some to her brothers. They were very hungry. They ate as they watched the countryside roll by. As the evening wore on, they grew tired. Hanna watched her brothers' heads bob up and down and their eyes close. The next thing she knew, it was morning.

The train made many stops. As they crossed into Germany, their papers were checked again. Finally, they arrived in Bremen. They got off the train and carried their bundles two blocks to a boardinghouse. Hanna was very tired.

Haskell knocked at the door. A large, pleasant woman opened the door. "I am Haskell Gorelik. Do you have room for my brother and sister and me for a few days? We shall be leaving on Wednesday on a ship for America."

"Come in. I am Mrs. Goldstein. If you don't mind sharing, I can put you two young men in a room with two other men. Your sister can share a room with Mrs. Krakov and her baby."

Hanna, Haskell, and Morris looked at each other, nodding in agreement. "That will be fine, Mrs. Goldstein." Haskell paid her for their rooms. Hanna was so proud of Haskell. He was taking charge, being the man of the family. He was only sixteen, but he was very mature for his age.

When Hanna got to her room, she found Mrs. Krakov caring for her baby.

"Hello. I am Hanna Astonovitsky. I shall be sharing your room."

"Hello. I am Leah Krakov, and this is my baby, Rachael."

Rachael started crying. Hanna watched Leah cuddle and pat her baby. Both Leah and Rachael had dark hair and eyes with thick, dark eyelashes.

Hanna said, "What a beautiful baby!" She thought to herself that Leah was not much older than she. When Rachael continued crying, Hanna asked, "Doesn't she feel well?"

"She is sick," Leah blurted out. "She is breaking out in a rash. Oh, I hope she won't be sick on the ship. We are meeting my husband in Galveston. He has never seen Rachael."

Hanna could tell she was nervous and scared. She looked grateful to have another woman to talk to.

"I shall be glad to help you with Rachael. I helped take care of my three younger brothers. I have experience with boy babies, but not girl babies." Hanna smiled at her.

"As far as I know, they all cry and want to be held. That would be wonderful if you could help me. Thank you, Hanna." Leah had a look of relief on her face. Hanna noticed her pretty smile changed her whole appearance.

The next two days were very cold. Hanna wanted to get out and walk around the town to see the ships. But whenever she stepped outside, the cold always drove her back inside.

Early Wednesday morning, Hanna woke to a loud banging at her door.

"Who is it?" Hanna asked.

"It is Morris. The ship is here. Get ready to go, quickly."

In a flash, Hanna and Leah were up and dressed. In just a few minutes they were standing at the door with all their bundles, saying goodbye to Mrs. Goldstein.

"Here is some fresh bread and fruit for your trip," said Mrs. Goldstein.

"Thank you," they all called as they rushed off.

The walk to the ship was only a few blocks, but there was a cold wind blowing which chilled Hanna to her bones. When they came in sight of the ship, Hanna stopped to read the name.

"Chemnitz," Hanna gasped. It was a steamship. *This is what Velvel must have felt when he saw it,* she thought to herself. She felt closer to him, knowing she was to cross the ocean on the same ship as Velvel.

They got in line to board the ship. The long line snaked on board and went down the stairs to the steerage compartment. It was dark, and there were many people crowded together. The sounds and smells came from every direction. Hanna heard Russian, German, Italian, Yiddish, and some languages she didn't know. She smelled fish, salami, fruits, vegetables, garlic, and onions.

Hanna and her brothers picked some bunks to the right of the door. They put their things away under the bunks and helped Leah get settled nearby. Then they all went up on deck. As they stood huddled together against the cold, the ship pushed off from the dock. Each person was lost in his own thoughts. They were on their way!

During the trip, little Rachael cried a lot. When Leah got tired, Hanna held Rachael and walked her back and forth until she quieted. Hanna thought, *How sweet a tiny baby is. But it is scary having another human being depend on you for everything.*

Haskell and Morris spent their time wandering all over the ship. They watched the crew check the emergency sails. They stood amazed watching the crew climb so high to adjust the sails.

"That looks like fun," said Morris.

"Would you want to climb the masts?" asked Haskell.

"Yes. Wouldn't you?" asked Morris.

"No. I want to get to America in one piece!" replied Haskell. They continued their walk, watching crewmen scrub the deck, put tools away, and tidy up.

"If the ship is as safe as it is clean, we shall get there in fine shape," said Haskell. Morris nodded in agreement.

Even though Hanna was shy, she had a natural curiosity about people. She passed her time by talking to many people who were traveling in steerage. She found that most of them were Jews. They were going to Fort Worth, Dallas, Houston, and many smaller towns where Jews had settled and were ready to help others. They were all looking for their future in America, the same as Hanna.

After three weeks on the rolling seas, Hanna was wondering if she would ever see land again. The trip had not been too bad, but the rolling of the ship and the boredom were taking their toll on Hanna.

Suddenly she heard, "Land ho!" The chant was picked up. "Land ho . . . Land ho!"

Everyone rushed up on deck and pressed against the railing. Sure enough, there was land off in the distance. Some people were saying, with wonder in their voices, "America, America." Some were saying prayers of thanks. Some were crying.

Haskell and Morris grabbed Hanna and held each other tightly. "We made it. We made it!" they cried.

The ship dropped anchor. Seagulls were swooping down to catch fish. Some people were throwing bits of bread and crackers to the birds. The seagulls glided past to catch them in midair.

How graceful they are, thought Hanna.

Haskell and Morris handed Hanna and Leah crusts of bread to throw to the seagulls. They threw them as high as they could. They all laughed when the birds caught them.

Hanna turned her eyes to shore. She was searching the crowd for Velvel. She couldn't find him. They joined the long line of people leaving the ship and walked down the long wooden plank to the pier. When Hanna stepped onto the pier, she was very wobbly from being on the ship for such a long time. It was a funny feeling. Hanna looked at Haskell and Morris, and they all held on to each other and laughed.

Hanna kept searching the faces of strangers. As they stood apart from the crowd, they saw people forming a circle around a well-dressed man.

Look how fine he is dressed, thought Hanna. She walked over to the edge of the crowd. "Who is this man?" she asked.

"That is Rabbi Henry Cohen," someone answered. "He speaks Yiddish. He is telling us where to go and what to do."

Rabbi Cohen motioned the group to follow him. He led them into a large building. Long lines of people snaked through the building, up one aisle and down another.

"Welcome to America, and welcome to Galveston, Texas," Rabbi Cohen said. "Please follow the lines. The officials will check your papers, your eyes, and your belongings. When you finish here, I shall meet you and we will go to the Jewish Immigrants Information Bureau. I know you are tired from your long journey. You will be able to rest soon."

Hanna had never seen such a modern rabbi. He had no beard, and he spoke English. She had heard about him on the ship. People said he met every ship carrying Jewish immigrants.

An official asked Hanna something. She couldn't understand what he was saying, but thought that he must want to know her name and where she was from. She was very frightened, but she replied, "I am Hanna Astonovitsky from Parichi, Russia." The official had her repeat it several times. Then he stamped her papers and motioned her to move along.

The next person looked at her eyes and had her read a Hebrew eyechart. She was passed along to a doctor, who quickly checked her over and listened to her heart.

Finally, an official opened her bundle and looked at her things: a samovar, candlesticks, feather bed, feather pillows, linens, pots and pans, and clothes. She tied her pack back into a knot and followed the line out the building.

Rabbi Cohen was waiting. Word passed down the line to follow him. She walked the two blocks to the Jewish Immigrants Information Bureau, all the time searching for Velvel.

Haskell said, "Don't worry. He will find us."

As they walked into the building, there were people waiting. A table held food and drinks. Before she had a chance to set her things down, someone grabbed her and swung her off her feet. It was Velvel. She dropped her bundles. They hugged and kissed, laughing and crying together. Haskell and Morris dropped their bundles, too, and hugged Velvel, pounding him on the back.

Velvel picked Hanna up and swung her around. "You are home, Hanna. You are home!" he cried.

18

A New Start

Hanna was writing her weekly letter to her family. A very great deal had happened to her since she last saw them. She told them all about her travels, by train, by ship, then by train again to Fort Worth. She wrote about her new friend, Leah Krakov:

Her baby, Rachael, had the measles and was sick the whole time we were on the ship. I helped comfort her as best I could. Such a sweet baby! I felt sorry for her. I just got a letter from Leah. She lives in a nearby city of Dallas. When we arrived in Galveston, Leah and Rachael were quarantined for a few days. When Rachael's bumps went away, they were allowed to join Mr. Krakov. I hope we shall be able to see them soon.

Hanna told her family about the Katzenbaums:

> When we arrived in Fort Worth, we went immediately to the home of Max and Rosa Katz. Their name used to be Katzenbaum. Many people shorten their names when they move here. We are thinking of doing this, too. It would be much easier for people to say Novit than Astonovitsky. The Katz' have a darling little girl, almost two years old, named Jenny. They are very nice to us. Rosa is helping me learn English. I have a little book. I write down all the words in it. There is so much to learn. I sometimes wonder if I shall ever learn it all!

One evening after supper, the men talked in the parlor while Hanna and Rosa put away the dishes.

"We have saved enough money for a pushcart. We need to start our business as soon as possible," Velvel said.

"I agree," said Max. "Where should we sell? There are pushcarts on all the busy corners in town."

"I have been thinking about that. We need to look at smaller towns nearby. We can get our bananas off the train, then split up and travel around, selling them. How does this sound to you?" asked Velvel.

"It sounds like a good idea to me. Let's take a ride into the country. Maybe we shall find just the right place to set up business," said Max.

"What is all this talk about a ride into the country?" asked Hanna. She and Rosa took off their aprons and hung them in the kitchen. They joined the men in the parlor.

"Would you ladies like to join us on Sunday?" asked Max.

"I think it could be arranged," replied Rosa with a wink at Hanna.

"Could you ladies prepare a picnic basket for us?" asked Velvel.

"That, too, could be arranged," said Hanna, returning a wink to Rosa.

Early the next morning, they took a rented buggy and horses north. They passed through many little towns with strange-sounding names . . . Haslet, Rhome, Decatur. They stopped by the side of the road to eat their picnic. Haskell and Morris spread the cloth on the ground. Hanna and Rosa spread out the food while they watched Jenny play. Velvel and Max tended to the horses. The day was crisp and cool, but the sun was bright in the sky.

"It is a lovely day for a picnic, don't you think?" Velvel said, taking a hard-boiled egg as Hanna put the bowl down on the cloth.

"In the old country we would never think of doing this in the winter. But here the sun warms you, even if the day is cold," said Hanna.

They ate the picnic lunch, loaded up the buggy, and continued their ride through the little towns.

What nice towns, Hanna thought. She waved at people they passed on the street. *They are friendly too.*

The others agreed. They found a boardinghouse

and the weary travelers went straight to bed. The next morning they arose refreshed and ready to continue.

During the long ride home, they discussed what they had seen.

"You want us to move to a tiny town where there are no Jews?" asked Hanna. "How will we be Jewish there?"

"We are Jews. We shall continue to be Jews," said Velvel.

"How can we be Jews with no *shul*?" asked Hanna.

"We don't need a *shul* to pray to God," answered Velvel. "You don't wear a *sheitel* like the married women in Russia did. Are you any less a Jew?"

"It is the modern way," answered Hanna. "You might not be able to keep *kosher,* traveling around."

"You will pack my lunch. I shall do the best I can," said Velvel.

"Will you travel on the *Shabbos*?" asked Hanna.

"Yes, if it is needed. God will forgive me."

"We came here to have the freedom to be Jews, but look what is happening. We are going to forget how to be Jews!" Hanna burst into tears.

"Hanna, what is wrong? Please don't cry. It is not so bad." Velvel was startled. He didn't know what to do.

"How can we raise our baby as a Jew when we are no longer practicing Jews?" Hanna cried.

"A baby? Hanna, are we going to have a baby?"

Velvel held his breath while he waited for her answer.

"I think so," Hanna said softly. "Oh, Velvel, I am so scared. We are so far away from our families and our home."

Velvel put his arms around Hanna and rocked her back and forth as if she were a baby. "We are a family now," he said, "and this is our home. This baby is part of our future and the reason we came to America. He will have a better life here than he ever could have had in Russia. Why, he could even grow up to be president of the United States! What do you think of that?" He drew back to look at Hanna.

"I think you are wrong. You are calling this baby 'he,' but I think it might be a 'she.'" Hanna smiled through her tears.

"Whatever it is, we shall give it the best life we can. It will be an American citizen," Velvel said proudly.

"I shall have a lot to write to Mama and Papa tomorrow." Hanna looked at Velvel, and they both nodded and laughed.

Glossary of Yiddish* Words

Bubbye (BU-bee): grandmother.

challah (KHAH-leh): braided loaf of bread for the Sabbath meal.

Chanukah (KHAH-ne-kuh): an eight-day Jewish festival of lights.

charoses (kha-RO-ses): mixture of apples, nuts, honey, and wine.

chazzan (KHA-zn): cantor, professional singer; assists the rabbi during services.

cheder (KHAY-der): Hebrew school.

chuppa (KHU-peh): wedding canopy.

dreidel (DRAY-del): Chanukah top.

gelt (GELT): money.

gribenehs (GRI-ben-ehs): fat from fowl cooked with onion.

kosher (KO-sher): fit to eat according to dietary laws.

latkes (LOT-kehs): potato pancakes.

matzo (MOTT-seh): unleavened bread served at Pesach.

matzo balls (MOTT-seh BALLS): dumplings made from matzo meal.

mazel tov (MOZ-z'l TUV): congratulations.

menorah (men-AW-ra): Chanukah candelabra.

moror (mo-ROAR): horseradish; bitter herb.

Pesach (PAY-sokh): Passover holiday.

Seder (SAY-der): combination meal and religious service the first night of Pesach.

Shabbos (SHAH-bes): Sabbath.

sheitel (SHY-tel):   wig worn by Jewish women after they were married.
shekel (SHEK-el):   Hebrew silver coin.
shul (SHUL):   synagogue; place of worship.
yeshiva (yeh-SHEE-va):   Hebrew college.
Zayde (ZAY-deh):   grandfather.

* Yiddish (YID-dish) is a language adapted by Jews from several languages, but mostly German.

Bibliography

Juvenile

Freedman, Russell. *Immigrant Kids*. New York: E. P. Dutton, 1980.

Adult

Eiseman, Alberta. *From Many Lands*. New York: Atheneum, 1970.

Howe, Irving. *World of Our Fathers*. New York: Harcourt Brace Jovanovich, Inc., 1976.

Marinbach, Bernard. *Galveston: Ellis Island of the West*. Albany: State University of New York Press, 1983.

Ornish, Natalie. *Pioneer Jewish Texans*. Dallas: Texas Heritage Press, 1989.

Potok, Chaim. *Wanderings, Chaim Potok's History of the Jews*. New York: Alfred A. Knopf, 1978.

Roskies, Diane K., and David G. Roskies. *The Shtetle Book*. KTAV Publishing House, Inc., 1975.

University of Texas Institute of Texan Cultures. *The Jewish Texans*. San Antonio, 1974.

Winegarten, Ruthe, and Cathy Schechter. *Deep in the Heart: The Lives and Legends of Texas Jews*. Austin: Eakin Press, 1990.

Zborowski, Mark, and Elizabeth Herzog. *Life Is With People: The Culture of the Shtetle*. New York: Schocken, 1952.

Films (Documentary)

Mondell, Allen, and Cynthia Salzman Mondell. *West of Hester Street*. Dallas, 1983.

Plays

Harelik, Mark. *The Immigrant, A Hamilton County Album*. New York: Available Press, Ballantine Books, 1985.

ABOUT THE AUTHOR

JAN SIEGEL HART's grandmother, Annie Harelik Novit, emigrated from Russia to Texas in 1909. Sixty years later she recorded her story about life in Russia and about her experiences as a newcomer in a strange land. The author transcribed these poignant audiotapes and created a story for parents and children alike. In addition to writing, the author is involved in a variety of volunteer activities. She also enjoys singing and theatre work. Mrs. Hart is available to speak to children or adult groups. She tells her story in costume as her grandmother, by request.